SALTY BABY

SUGAR BABIES #4

CHARITY PARKERSON

--Warning: This book is intended for readers over the age of 18.

Copyright © 2019 Charity Parkerson
Editor: BZ Hercules & Consultants
ISBN: 978-1-946099-56-3

INTRODUCTION

THIS ISN'T LOVE, BUT THEIR FEELINGS ARE JUST AS INTENSE AND UNWAVERING. IT'S HATE... MAYBE.

Falcon's best friend used to date the world's biggest nightmare. Mason is conceited, self-serving, and out for only himself. Falcon hates him. He'll do anything to keep Mason away from Dillion. That's how Falcon ends up a guest at a weekend destination wedding he has no desire to attend, but he can't let Dillion go alone. It's a plan that seems perfect until Mason ends up in the wrong bed.

There was a time when Mason would have gone to any length to get Dillion back. Now he's just trying to get through this wedding with his pride intact. It's a hope that's dashed the minute he makes a wrong turn on the way to his room. Or did he?

With no chance of ever being with Dillion again, Mason tries moving on, but the direction he's headed seems every bit as doomed. Even though Falcon hates him, he keeps coming around. Each time Mason finds himself in Falcon's company, it seems like the world is conspiring to throw them together. Except the truth is a bit more lurid, and their secret has them in real danger of losing everyone they care about.

PROLOGUE

PRESENT DAY...

THE INCESSANT RINGING wouldn't stop. Falcon rolled over, blinking at the clock, or rather where he thought the clock should be. He traveled so much, he had a horrible time remembering where he was. The ringing stopped before immediately starting again.

"For the love of all things holy, make it stop."

Falcon snatched up the phone as the growled words rumbled next to his ear. Dillion's name flashed across the face. His heart rate kicked up. There was no good reason why Dillion would call nonstop in the middle of the night.

"Hello?" Even to Falcon's ears, his voice sounded slurred.

"Falcon. I need help."

1

Falcon sat up—wide awake. "What's wrong?"

Dillion sniffed. Everything inside Falcon went on high alert. "Beck woke up in the middle of the night in horrible pain and I brought him to the ER. They immediately took him into surgery and now I'm just a wreck."

Falcon threw off his blankets and stood. "I'm on my way." His mind raced. Would it be quicker if he drove or flew? Fuck. What town was this again? A sexy green stare held his—silent and waiting to learn the issue. Vegas. He was at home in Vegas. "Let me look at flights. It might be quicker if I drive." He rubbed his forehead. "Damn. That would take like ten hours. Let me see which way would get me there the quickest and I'll be there. Okay? Just hang on."

"Falcon, I'm scared."

He sat. His knees gave out at the confession. Why did he always stay so far away from Dillion? Warm lips brushed his shoulder, offering silent comfort. "I'm on my way. I promise, baby."

"Okay. I'll see you soon."

Falcon disconnected the call and started looking for a flight. He booked the earliest one he could find.

"Is everything okay?"

At the question, Falcon twisted and looked behind him. "I don't know." He took a breath, trying to decide what to say. "It's... Sorry. I have to go to Aspen."

Mason's mouth lifted in one corner. "You can say his name, you know? I won't start foaming at the mouth with unrequited desire."

Fuck. Falcon didn't know what to do. "I know you're supposed to be here for a while. If you want, you can fly back with me."

Mason dropped his gaze to his lap, hiding his feelings the way he always did. "No. I think I'll stay. Surely there's a cheap hotel room nearby. I might as well enjoy my vacation."

Ugh. Falcon shifted to his knees and straddled Mason's lap, knocking him onto his back. "Stay here. No matter what, I'll be back by Tuesday. Okay?"

The hope in Mason's eyes tightened Falcon's chest. "Okay. Don't you need to go?" Even as Mason posed the question, he massaged Falcon's ass between his hands.

"Not yet. I have a couple of hours to waste with you. Let's make it count." Damn. This would all blow up in his face very soon. Falcon felt it in his gut. The thing was, Falcon wasn't so sure he cared anymore.

ONE

TWO MONTHS EARLIER...

This was the gayest wedding Mason had ever attended, and that opinion came from the bottom of his rainbow-colored soul. His co-worker, Summer, and her fiancée Autumn had outdone themselves. Since Autumn's family had completely disowned her for "choosing an alternative lifestyle" over family, and over half of Summer's family booted her too, the pair had decided to make this the most pride-filled wedding ever seen. They had pulled it off, to Mason's mind. All the bridesmaids were dudes and all the best men were chicks and everyone wore a different shade of pastel, turning the entire ceremony into a rainbow explosion. Truly, it had been beautiful. Not that Mason had seen a damn thing from the moment he had spotted Dillion. Since Dillion had been the first to come down the aisle, wearing a pink and poofy dress, that had been the end of ceremony-watching for Mason. His gaze hadn't budged.

Dillion was so different now from when they had been dating. He wore dresses and heels with pride. Everything Dillion had once been in private for only Mason's eyes, he proudly owned for the world now. Mason missed him like crazy. He didn't try to talk to Dillion anymore. It was pointless. Mason was banned from Incubus on Friday nights so Dillion could visit without seeing him. Not that Dillion went anywhere without his new man. When Dillion wasn't accompanied by Beck, his best friend Falcon took over. It was as if they thought Mason would abduct the man if they turned their backs. Mason might be a bad person, but he wasn't that bad.

Since very few of Summer's family members attended the wedding and none of Autumn's family had, Mason and Summer's boss, Trace, had decided he would foot the bill and give the pair the destination wedding of their dreams. That was how Mason ended up sitting here in the most gorgeous place he had ever been in his life. Without Trace paying his way, Mason wouldn't ever see this town again. Trace had rented a huge mansion in White Mountains, New Hampshire. The view was breathtaking. And still, Mason couldn't look away from Dillion. All through dinner and nonstop free drinks, his eyes never budged. He tried not to be creepy about it, but the more he drank, the harder it was to stop himself from crossing the room—Falcon or no Falcon to stop him. He wasn't sure what kept him glued in his seat. Maybe, in his heart, Mason knew Dillion was better off now. That didn't stop him from staring. It didn't help that the way the tables had been set up in a horseshoe fashion had Mason facing the guy. He hadn't been in charge of the seating arrangements. Apparently, some masochist had. Mason wasn't sure he was in charge of his eyes any longer either. No amount of internal screaming forced his gaze away from the only person he had ever loved.

"You look really gorgeous, Mason. Thank you so much for being here."

Mason tore his eyes away from Dillion and focused on Summer. She looked happy. Her blond hair shimmered in the chandelier lighting. The sleeveless dress she wore matched her light blue eyes to perfection. He flashed her a smile and tried not slur his words. It was possible he had a bit too much alcohol flowing in his veins. "You look beautiful. Happiness suits you."

Summer kissed his cheek. She swiped at his cheek, wiping away her lipstick. "I know it's not easy for you to be here. Two-thirds of my family couldn't be bothered, so I really appreciate you going the extra mile."

"We're friends." That was all that mattered. It was Summer's day. He was pretty good at ruining things, but he would behave for her.

She squeezed his arm. Her gaze dropped to his bicep. She laughed and squeezed his arm again. "Jesus, dude. You're solid. How much time do you spend at the gym?"

He snorted. "Surely you don't think I pay my bills by working the door at Incubus. I'm also a personal trainer."

"Huh. Seems like I should've known that."

Mason shrugged. "I guess I don't really talk about it, so why would you?" Mason looked around, searching for a way to change the subject. No one knew him. He liked it that way. Mason fought the urge to look toward Dillion's seat. A wave of sadness washed over him. At one time, he had shown himself to Dillion. No one else had ever gotten so deep. "I think I'll head to my room. That open bar has been way too good to me tonight." The alcohol made him weak.

Summer rubbed his arm. "All right. Be careful heading up. That side of the house is like a maze."

Mason nodded. He had already gotten lost twice on trips to his room and he had been sober then. The last thing he wanted was to end up wandering the hallways all night.

.

Damn, Falcon hated weddings. No doubt there was some deep psychological reason—like he knew he would never have this or whatever. His reasons didn't matter any more than his hatred. Dillion had asked him to come. There was nothing Falcon wouldn't do to make Dillion happy. They had been friends for as long as Falcon had memories. Lots of people had come and gone from his life, including his parents. Despite finding fame and money, things other people liked to circle like vultures, Falcon wasn't a people person. Dillion was the one with the winning personality. Falcon was the one who growled, hissed, and scratched. He drove people away. Dillion was always the exception.

Thankfully, the actual ceremony flew and then

the alcohol flowed freely. "How late do we have to stay?"

Dillion glanced over at Falcon's question. "You don't have to stay at all, babe. I understand if you want to go out and be free. I just hoped to steal you away for a weekend and spend some time with you. Are you okay?"

Falcon shrugged. He was in a shit mood. The last thing he wanted was to take it out on Dillion. "I shouldn't be feeling any pain, but my head is pounding. We can stay if you want. There's nothing else to do in this town. I thought about going to bed early, but I probably won't be able to sleep anyhow."

Dillion made a dismissive motion. "I'll give you a couple of my sleeping pills. They're prescription. You'll be out in no time."

Falcon leaned back in his chair and swept the room with his gaze. "Finish your drink, angel. Don't worry over me."

Dillion patted his thigh beneath the table and leaned Beck's way. Beck touched his lips to Dillion's ear. Falcon looked away. Sometimes, it was hard being around people in love. Falcon's gaze landed on a familiar figure across the room. Mason was impossible to miss. He was a solid mountain of muscle who also stood a foot taller than everyone else. Falcon was hardly the only person looking Mason's way. If Mason noticed, he didn't let on. He sat talking with the bride, ignoring the coveted glances. Falcon wondered if Mason was really oblivious or if he was so accustomed to being wanted by everyone that he expected all eyes to be on him. The funny thing was, if Falcon had to guess, he would say Mason was clueless. He looked sad, even when he smiled. Falcon polished off his Crown and Coke, trying not to look too closely at why he cared.

Dillion dug a couple of pills from his bag and passed them Falcon's way. "All right, babe. Get lost. I know you're sick of babysitting me."

"You've got Beck for that," Falcon said, accepting the pills. "I'm just here to drink, steal your time, and get a free vacation."

Dillion chuckled. The sound made Falcon smile. "As if you can't afford to go wherever you want and don't already travel nonstop. Don't play coy. I know the two of you put your heads together and decided I couldn't be alone this weekend."

It was hard, considering his growing migraine, but Falcon kept his face blank. "I have no idea what you're talking about. You're a grown man."

Dillion pursed his lips and side-eyed him.

"Mhmm. Yeah. Okay. Whatever you say. Get gone. Beck is about to seduce me, so your duties are over."

Beck winked but stayed silent. That one gesture was Beck in a nutshell. He was the strong, silent, and supporting love of Dillion's life. Falcon couldn't have picked a better man for Dillion if he had created the man from scratch. He was exactly the calm and loving man Dillion needed to offset his anxieties. They were perfect together. Beautiful. Falcon felt... alone. It was ugly, and he didn't know how to stop. So he walked away before he did something stupid.

As Summer walked away, moving on to speak to the next guest, Mason lost the battle against himself. His gaze slid Dillion's direction. His entire entourage was gone. There was definitely no reason for him to keep hanging around and drinking now. Maybe he would drag the chair in his bedroom onto the balcony and enjoy the night air. He needed to breathe.

Mason gave himself a mental pat on the back when he found his room on the first try. It was so dark, he couldn't see a damn thing. The open curtains let the moonlight in, keeping him from breaking his neck on the way to the bed. Mason froze at the foot of the bed. There was an outline of a person beneath the covers. Mason cast a desperate look around the room, searching for anything familiar. Had he accidentally made a wrong turn after all? All these fucking rooms looked alike, and since it wasn't a hotel, there were no locked doors or hotel keys. Shit. He recognized the chair by the French doors, and he was pretty sure he had left those curtains open. That was his view. Right? Goddamn it. He couldn't tell.

The lump in the bed moved. Mason considered hitting the floor. Then, a tuft of dark brown hair appeared above the sheets. Mason's breath caught. It was Dillion. He was alone. Why was he alone? Longing hit like a truck from nowhere, stealing the air from his lungs. Had Dillion sneaked into his room and fallen asleep while waiting for him? Damn it. Just when he thought he might survive the loss, Dillion always came back. Mason couldn't resist him. He set one knee on the mattress and held his breath. Dillion didn't stir. Mason snagged the edge of the blanket and slowly dragged it down Dillion's body. He wished he could see, but he didn't want to startle Dillion awake. Dillion was the only person Mason loved more than himself. The hope growing in his chest was crushing his lungs. Without warning, Dillion shot from the bed and the bedside lamp flared to life.

Falcon stood nude and blinking at Mason. "Mason?"

Goddamn. He was gorgeous. Mason had a hard time looking at the man's face. Holy shit. The man's entire body looked like it had been chiseled from marble. "Um. I thought you were Dillion."

The confusion in Falcon's expression cleared away. "Oh. I see. You came to get fucked."

Mason shifted, feeling a bit exposed. He imagined that was exactly how it looked. "Not really, no. I thought this was my room."

"Strip."

His mind went blank. "I'm sorry."

Falcon's flat expression never shifted. "I know you are. Strip."

Mason blinked. "I'm... confused."

"You came to get fucked. Dillion is taken. He's in bed with Beck right now, getting everything you could never give him. They're getting married soon. You're never getting another chance. That's just the way of things. If you didn't come here to get fucked, get out." Falcon climbed back into bed as if Mason wasn't there, confusing the fuck out of him. It was odd. Nothing Falcon said about Dillion bothered him. It seemed, somewhere in this house, Dillion was in bed with Beck, and Mason didn't mind. There was a different sexy man here in this bed. Falcon hadn't physically thrown Mason out the way Mason knew he could. Mason stood, trying to decide what to do. His gaze slid to the nude vision Falcon presented. Wow. He was all sleek muscle and huge cock. Mason peeled off his shirt. Fuck it. He was drunk enough not to care. He could regret things tomorrow when he was sober. Mason wasn't the type to deny himself when an opportunity presented itself. He was too drunk to question things.

Mason dug a condom from his wallet before he finished stripping. It was lubricated, which made it taste funny, but Mason didn't do anything at all without some sort of barrier. At least, he tried not to. Dillion had been an exception to a lot of things. Nonetheless, Falcon wasn't sweet and innocent like Dillion. He was caustic and undeniably wicked. No doubt he had fucked hundreds of people. Mason planned to bring his A game. Falcon didn't watch him strip. He kept his arm slung over his eyes, as if he didn't care if Mason stayed or went. Falcon wasn't the type to be impressed by just anyone. If Mason were a better person or sober, he might have questioned why Falcon wanted this at all. The problem was, Mason currently felt zero pain and just fuck it. It wasn't like it was his first one-night stand.

Mason crawled onto the foot of the bed and leaned in. He pressed his lips to Falcon's thigh as he fumbled to tear open the condom. A gasp shot through the room. Falcon's fingers found Mason's hair. He tugged, making Mason's scalp sting as he urged Mason toward his dick. Mason scrambled to roll the condom down Falcon's length as quickly as possible. He didn't feel the least bit in control of this encounter. Mason barely had time to cover Falcon's cock before Falcon shoved his dick in Mason's mouth. It was oddly hot being at someone's mercy. Mason was every bit as solid as Summer accused. He rarely met anyone who could manhandle him. While Falcon wasn't a big guy, he was quick, strong, and talented. He was a mixed martial arts expert who fought for a living. Several months ago, he had also handed Mason his ass when Mason had been trying to win back Dillion. Falcon had already proven he could control Mason if he wanted.

This was the only way Mason could best Falcon. He could make the man helpless with his mouth. Mason used his every skill against Falcon, taking him deep and making him writhe. Falcon moaned as he moved restlessly beneath Mason's ministrations. Mason's cock jumped and leaked at Falcon's open pleasure. In his haze of lust, Mason reached down and stroked himself. He needed relief. Falcon was sexy as hell.

In a flash of movement, everything spun. Mason fought the pillows on the bed as he found his face buried among them. His alcohol-soaked brain had a hard time grasping the change of scenery. Teeth sank into his back. Mason sucked in a gasp. Without warning, a cock filled his ass. Mason scratched at the sheets below him. He hadn't been prepared. While Mason was versatile, he hadn't bottomed for anyone in a damn long time. He certainly hadn't intended to end up here tonight. Mason sucked air and tried to relax. The only thing saving him was Falcon had gone completely still.

"Goddamn," Falcon breathed, kissing his shoulder. "I wasn't expecting you to be this goddamn tight. You're killing me."

Mason's muscles relaxed. His lust skyrocketed. Something about pleasing a man who absolutely loathed him was empowering as hell. Mason wanted Falcon to crave him long after he was gone. He wanted Falcon to think of him in the shower and be incapable of stopping himself from jerking off to this memory. Mason wanted Falcon to burn with shame for this night. Using his strength against Falcon, Mason pushed upward and flexed his muscles. A loud gasp vibrated against his back. Mason did it again, fucking the mattress every bit as much as he fucked Falcon.

Falcon's hands covered his. His fingers linked with Mason's. Warm lips skimmed his throat, and that was the last sweet gesture Mason received before Falcon took charge. He pounded inside Mason while kissing and biting every place he could reach. Mason fought for air as he openly fucked the bed and gave back as hard as he took it. There was nothing quick about their encounter. It seemed to go on forever. When Mason's orgasm finally hit, he swore he blacked out for a moment. He had never been more thoroughly fucked. Everything ached, even as he shook in ecstasy. If Falcon came, Mason missed it. Darkness swallowed him until there was nothing.

FALCON KEPT HIS SUNGLASSES FIRMLY IN PLACE and prayed his head wouldn't split in two. Jesus, he felt like death. The smell of the breakfast buffet being provided made his stomach churn. His entire body ached like someone had taken a baseball bat to him.

Dillion's sexy light green gaze lifted from his plate. He froze with a piece of fruit halfway to his mouth. "Holy shit. What happened to you? You look like you've been in a wreck."

"Thanks, sexy. I love you too." He didn't give Dillion time to feel guilty. Falcon realized he was the one in the bad mood. "I took those two sleeping pills you gave me on top of drinking too much." He shrugged as he dropped into the chair at Dillon's side. "I think I died."

"Did you just say you took both of those pills on top of drinking last night?"

Falcon stole a triangle of toast from Dillion's plate. "Yeah."

"Holy crap, Falcon. You were only supposed to take one. I gave you two so you'd have enough for the whole weekend. You're lucky you didn't die."

"It's too soon to judge. I still might keel over." Falcon meant the words from the bottom of his hungover soul.

A familiar scent assailed him. Falcon automatically turned his head. His gaze landed on Mason. An image slammed into Falcon. Those large muscles bunched and rolled. Mason grasped the sheets. The sexiest moan Falcon had ever heard caressed his ears. The moment was gone as quickly as it struck, but Falcon couldn't look away. Shit.

Mason turned his head, glancing over his shoulder as someone called his name. A deep maroon hickey marred his skin. Falcon's stomach cramped. Another flash of sucking Mason's neck as an orgasm claimed his body flitted across Falcon's brain. He couldn't breathe.

"I'll be right back." Without waiting for Dillion to acknowledge his words, Falcon practically flew from the room, chasing after Mason. He found him inside the dining room where the buffet sat, ordering an orange juice from the makeshift bar. Falcon didn't waste a second. He slid into the empty spot beside Mason. "What the fuck happened last night?"

Mason glanced over and eyed him for a moment. He didn't seem the least bit surprised by Falcon's question. That wasn't good. "Good morning to you too, Falcon. I see you plan to play the too-drunk-to-remember-anything card. No worries. I've had to do the same in the past."

"Dear God. It wasn't a dream." The hoarse whisper sounded horrified, even to Falcon's ears.

Mason eyed him for a moment longer. He shook his head, grabbed his orange juice, and walked away.

Falcon chased after him. He snagged the back of the man's t-shirt and hauled him through a side door, leading outside. The moment they were alone, Falcon went toe to toe with him. "I'm not fucking playing here, Mason. I need you to tell me what happened."

Mason rubbed his forehead and blew out a sigh. When he dropped his hand and focused on Falcon, he looked every bit as wrecked as Falcon felt. "You were in my bed when I went back to my room last night. I thought maybe I'd made a wrong turn, but when I woke up, all my stuff was there. So it had to be you who made the mistake."

"I think we're both aware we made a fucking mistake, but ending up in the wrong bed doesn't automatically mean sex, so what the fuck?"

To Mason's credit, he didn't smirk. "I guess you hammered the nail in the coffin, ensuring I can never win Dillion back, in the best way you knew how."

Falcon went cold. His face hardened. He felt it happen. It was out of his control. "No. Dillion can never, ever, never ever ever find out about that. Understood? I was full of alcohol and sleeping pills. Otherwise, that never would have happened."

Mason's eyes turned hard in a way Falcon had never seen. "If you're trying to claim I took advantage of you, you'd better back up a fucking second. You were in my bed. You are the one who propositioned me. Not the other way around. You."

Oh, goddamn. There was not a soul who could doubt him. Mason was telling the truth. Falcon swallowed—hard. "That doesn't leave here." Even Falcon heard the way his voice shook. Dillion was all he had. If Mason ruined that, Falcon wouldn't have anyone.

"I think I'll go find a microphone to make the announcement."

Falcon blinked. He would kill him.

Mason snorted. "Get the fuck over yourself. I'm not telling anyone. I'm a grown-ass man. Not a gossipy teen." With an angry scowl still in place, Mason tried stepping around him. Falcon snagged his arm before he could get away.

Falcon took a sharp breath. "I didn't do anything to hurt you, right? Like you were totally in, right?"

Mason's face cleared. His gaze moved over Falcon's face. "I made my choices. You should go back to Dillion before he sees you with me." Mason didn't sound angry. In fact, he just seemed sad. Falcon spent a moment questioning why he was such a bad person on the inside where no one could see—why he always wanted things he shouldn't.

Falcon dipped his chin and headed for the door. He needed to get back to Dillion. If he made it through this weekend with their friendship intact, Falcon planned to disappear for a while. Otherwise, he might succeed in self destructing.

"Falcon."

Falcon froze at the deep unhappiness in Mason's tone. He glanced over his shoulder to where he had left Mason standing.

Mason pulled a face. "I'm cool with pretending this never happened. If I hadn't been drunk, I never would have let you put your friendship with Dillion at risk. You're all he has. So it never happened."

It was funny. Falcon hadn't thought it possible for him to be an even bigger piece of shit in this scenario. In the face of Mason's open hurt, Falcon realized he didn't deserve to have friends.

TWO

TWO WEEKS LATER...

Trace stared at him like he didn't know what to say. All Mason felt was relieved. He had been hired at Incubus before the club opened. Since that time, Mason had been promoted to manager from a bouncer and then demoted again. It was long past the time he should have left. In truth, Mason didn't know why he had stayed after losing his management position. Hope springing eternal, he supposed. There had always been a part of him that believed Dillion would come back. Now he knew it didn't matter if Dillion ever wanted him again, so he was done.

"You've been with me since day one," Trace said, finding his tongue. "Tell me what you need to stay."

A sad smile tugged at Mason's lips. He supposed this was another reason why he had stayed so long. Mason liked Trace. It wasn't like Mason didn't understand the demotion had been his fault. He had been a different person since meeting Dillion—crazy. Reckless. That was the gist of things. That was why he needed to leave. Mason didn't recognize himself any longer. "Nothing. It's time for me to move on. A guy from my gym is looking for work. He can replace me right away, if you're willing. I've known David for a while. He's hard—"

"Is this because of the stuff with Dillion?" Trace asked, cutting him off mid-speech.

An image of the way Falcon had looked at him before walking away in New Hampshire flashed through Mason's mind. He hadn't stopped thinking about Falcon's devastation since. Part of Mason wondered if he had accepted Falcon's offer just to see that look, wiping away all the times Falcon had kept him from Dillion. He didn't know, and that mattered. Not knowing meant there was a real possibility that was exactly why he had crawled into that bed. Mason didn't like who he had become since he started working here.

"Your silence is answer enough."

Mason shook his head, forcing his brain on task.

25

"No. This is just a young man's life and I'm getting old. When I started working here, I was just out of a ten-year relationship and this job seemed like a perfect fuck you to him while making extra money. Now I'm tired."

Trace's shoulders expanded as he took a deep breath. "Well, if you ever need a job, you'll always have a place here. I truly appreciate all your hard work."

A hint of sadness wormed its way into Mason's relief. Trace had been more than good to Mason. "I'll miss everyone."

"I hope you plan to still come by and visit."

"Of course." Even as Mason agreed, it felt like a lie. Mason wasn't only tired from the late nights. He was also burned out from the drama and flirting. The crowds made him lonelier than being alone.

After clearing away the final details, a few more promises to visit and stay in touch, Mason made his way back out to the main floor to finish up his last night of closing duties. With each passing moment, his depression grew. He knew he should make the rounds, letting everyone know it was his last night, Mason withdrew further inside himself. As the last of the club's closing crowd made their way out,

Mason spotted a familiar face among the wave —Falcon.

Mason's mind skipped a beat. He didn't think he had seen Falcon among the partiers tonight. How had the man slipped inside and avoided him all night? Falcon usually drew a crowd by his presence alone. Of course, Mason was equally surprised he spotted the guy. He wore a ball cap down low and wasn't drawing any attention his way. It was like Mason was tuned in to the man, picking him out a sea of exiting faces. For some reason he couldn't explain, Mason's muscles flexed—like he fought the urge to chase him. That was dumb. Mason turned away. No doubt Falcon had intentionally hidden from him. Mason hadn't noticed if Dillion had been with him. Odd.

Mason shook his head and made himself useful. More hands made less work and that meant he could get home faster. He tried hard not to think about Falcon. Just as he had done since leaving New Hampshire, Mason swung between self-loathing, anger, and sadness. He was mad at himself for messing with Falcon. Disappointed in life in general. His whole life, Mason had worked hard and pulled his weight. He had tried hard to be a good person for more years than not. It didn't seem to matter how he behaved; things never changed for him. He was still broke, struggling, and alone. It was exhausting work hating himself.

Mason's black mood carried him through the final minutes of working. When he hit the parking lot, he spotted the cops right away. That wasn't unusual. There was always someone who left at closing time drunk and ready to drive. What shocked Mason was that it was Falcon being questioned. He stood inside the open door of a Hellcat. It looked as if things were turning heated. Judging by the drunk lean Falcon had going on, there was only one way Falcon was leaving here at this rate—in the backseat of a police car.

Without thought, Mason raced to intervene. "Whoa. Hold up, Steve. He's not driving. He's getting his stuff to come home with me."

The cop, who was a regular at Incubus when off duty, looked between Mason and Falcon and back again. "All right. As long as you don't let him drive anywhere."

Mason kept his most flirtatious smile locked in place. "He won't. I promise. He's just been waiting for me to get finished up here."

Steve nodded. "I'll wait in the car and make sure

you two get safely from the parking lot." In other words, he planned to watch to be sure Mason was telling the truth. He couldn't let Falcon drive. Not that he would.

"Thanks for looking out for us," Mason said, still smiling. Being upbeat and naughty was how Mason survived. He had nothing else going for him.

"Fuck, I forgot you worked here," Falcon growled the moment Steve was out of earshot.

Mason rolled his eyes. "Yeah, yeah. Lock your car and let's go."

Falcon closed his door and immediately stumbled. Mason snagged Falcon around the waist and headed for his truck.

"Where are you taking me?"

"My place." No way would he show up at Dillion's with Falcon, even if he was saving the guy. He couldn't risk leaving him alone in a hotel. Falcon might die of alcohol poisoning or call a cab to take him back to his car.

"Trying to molest me again, huh? I don't blame you. Who can resist all this?" Falcon asked, drunkenly motioning toward himself.

"Damn, you're conceited." Even Mason heard the laughter in his own voice.

An ugly-sounding snort escaped Falcon. "I know

you, the middle-aged guy who focuses on nothing else but his own body and ensuring he never fucks anyone over the age of twenty-two, didn't just call me conceited."

Mason shook his head, wondering why he was bothering with Falcon. He should just dump the dude right here and leave him for the cops. "God, you're an asshole."

Falcon scoffed. "You're just now figuring this out? I'm a combative person. Why do you think I fight for a living? I don't like anyone." Falcon stumbled as he made the claim, forcing Mason to keep him upright.

Mason kept up his end of the conversation like nothing happened. "You have a lot of friends for someone who doesn't like anyone."

A low and sexy-sounding chuckle caressed Mason's ears as he helped Falcon into the passenger side of his truck. "I have one friend, and another because he's in love with that one. And if that second guy ever hurts my one and only friend, he'll be gone too. But I get what you're saying. I amend my original statement. I like one person. That's it. Fuck. Two people. My manager, Brett, is an okay guy."

Mason worked on buckling Falcon's seat belt like

the guy was a two-year-old. "In your defense, Dillion is impossible to dislike. I've been trying for a long time, so you can't really escape that."

"I see you're still pining after that one," Falcon said, dropping his head back against the seat and sounding ready to pass out.

Mason froze. His gaze moved over Falcon's face. "No."

Falcon's head lifted. Their gazes met. Sexy blue eyes stared at him, making him feel like Falcon could see into his soul. The truck's soft lighting haloed Falcon's dark hair, making Mason wonder where the hat he had been wearing earlier had gone. He looked wicked and untouchable with his hair a tousled mess.

"Good," Falcon said, sounding damnably sober. "He's too soft for you. I know you don't want to hear it or believe it, but you were doing real damage to someone who didn't deserve it."

"I know." Mason closed the door before he confessed any more of his sins. No one understood what falling for Dillion had been like for him. They had met at a nightclub where everyone should have been over eighteen. He hadn't learned Dillion was only seventeen until he was sick with obsession and nude. Dillion fucked with Mason's mind. Made him question his morality. Sometimes, Mason had hated Dillion every bit as much as he had loved him. Not that it mattered anymore.

Mason climbed behind the wheel. He didn't look Falcon's way. There was nothing Mason could ever say that would make Falcon think better of him. He wouldn't try.

"Thank you."

Mason's head whipped around at the quietly spoken words.

Falcon held his stare. "I appreciate you keeping me from going to jail."

Despite his best efforts, Mason couldn't find his voice. Never in a million years had he expected to get a thank you from Falcon. He sounded genuine too— like a different person. "You're welcome." Really, Mason had nothing else.

"No molesting me when I pass out, though. That's not cool."

A smile tugged at Mason's lips. He started the truck. Now Falcon sounded like himself again. He managed to hold his tongue for all of five minutes. Almost all the way to his house. It had to be some sort of record for restraint on his part. "First off, I thought you were Dillion. Secondly, I had no idea you were drugged out of your mind. Lastly, and this is the biggest of them all, you could've stopped me at any point before you ended up molesting me, but you didn't. Not that I blame you." He tossed Falcon a quick wink. "I'm very good at giving head."

"Who's conceited now?"

"It's not bragging if it's true," Mason said, pulling into his driveway. He would miss living so close to work. Mason pushed the button on his key fob to open the garage door before pulling inside.

Falcon didn't respond until Mason circled the truck and tried unsnapping his seatbelt. "To be fair, I was drugged out of my mind, so I don't really remember the blowjob. Of course, not remembering it implies it was subpar."

A snort of laughter escaped Mason. "Despite what you think, I do recognize when I'm being goaded."

"Can you?" Without warning, Mason found himself hauled forward. Falcon's mouth covered his. Everything inside Mason's mind screeched to a stop. His body took over. He had been kissed by countless men over the years. Mason had never, ever been kissed like Falcon did. It was sexy and domineering. Falcon took control and left no doubt he would stay in charge. His teeth sank into Mason's bottom lip, tugging. He licked and sucked, making Mason so hard, he felt lightheaded from the immediate rush of blood to his cock. As if Falcon knew, he made quick work of Mason's zipper. His hand dove inside Mason's jeans.

Mason needed more. He was immediately back in New Hampshire, incapable of saying no. "Come inside," Mason begged. He had to get Falcon nude again. He had rung this bell once. There was no reason now not to do it again. Falcon had fire. Mason wanted to get burned by him again.

Falcon chuckled against Mason's lips. Mason's stomach muscles clenched at the evil sound. "No. You're the one who's been bragging. Put your mouth to work or go away. I don't remember last time. Make sure I can't forget."

Mason was up for the challenge, but he also wasn't a pushover. If Falcon wanted a doormat, he should go elsewhere. "I'll rock your goddamn world," Mason swore, hearing the confidence in his own words. "But I'm not sucking dick in my garage when I have a perfectly good bed in the house."

Falcon stroked Mason's cock. Mason's resolve wavered. Falcon eyed him. "I thought you lived with someone."

With his dick in Falcon's hand, Mason was slow on the uptake. "Yeah. A roommate." It hit Mason. He pushed Falcon's hand away and zipped his pants. "Did you really think I would invite you to my bed if I had a live-in lover?"

Falcon turned sideways, leaving Mason no other choice but to take a step back. Before Mason's temper cooled, Falcon snagged the hem of Mason's t-shirt and wound it tighter until he lured Mason to stand to between his knees. He didn't look contrite, but Mason's irritation slipped away beneath the heat in Falcon's stare. "Invite me in again."

For a moment, Mason considered getting back behind the wheel and taking Falcon straight to Dillion. No doubt, that was the smart move. The right move. But Falcon looked at him in a way no one else had in a long time—like he saw past Mason's mask and wanted him anyway. Mason should run. He never saved himself when he should.

"I have a perfectly good bed inside. We should use it."

What a fool he always was.

FALCON HAD NO IDEA WHAT HE WAS DOING WITH Mason. He should have gone to Dillion's the minute he got to town. Instead, he had gone to Incubus. For hours, he had stood in the corner near a bartender he didn't recognize. His gaze had found Mason and hadn't budged. While tossing back shots and silently watching, Falcon had come to one major conclusion. Mason was unhappy. When people spoke to him, Mason smiled, but it wasn't real. When he was visibly lost in thought, Mason looked tired and done. Even with those revelations tucked under his belt, Falcon had left without making himself known. It hadn't been his intention to end up here. In fact, he wasn't sure he shouldn't leave. He didn't.

Instead, his grip tightened on Mason's shirt. His mouth watered in anticipation as Mason obeyed his silent command and lowered his head. Falcon's lips touched the corner of Mason's mouth. Neither of them moved. Mason's hands moved from where they rested on Falcon's thighs. He cupped Falcon's face. Then, the world tilted, and Falcon found himself staring at the garage floor. A burst of laughter popped from his lips before he could stop it. It was rare for anyone to get the drop on him. If he wanted, he could retake control of the situation. Hanging from Mason's shoulder as the man headed inside wasn't where he had expected to end up tonight. Falcon didn't fight it. All the thoughts he should have been considering didn't make an appearance. He was enjoying himself.

From his spot on Mason's shoulder, Falcon didn't get a good look at the darkened house. Mason didn't turn on any lights as he went. Plus, Falcon was oddly fascinated by the man's round ass. Falcon liked pointing out that Mason was over forty, but his ass was better than anyone's Falcon had ever seen. He was in the perfect spot to enjoy it.

The world tilted again as Falcon went flying. He landed with a small bounce on the mattress before a huge body covered him. The bed smelled like Mason's cologne. That was the only thing Falcon noticed before Mason's mouth covered his. Falcon was warm in Mason's hold—like he was cocooned in muscle. Mason massaged and rubbed. His tongue toyed with Falcon's as he rocked against Falcon, making him hotter by the second. Since their night together in New Hampshire, Falcon hadn't stopped feeling like they had made a huge mistake. Now he couldn't wait to make it again.

Falcon dragged Mason's shirt upward until Mason leaned away long enough to let him have it. He worked on the button of Mason's jeans next. The man's thighs were so thick with muscle that his jeans were baggy in the waist, making them easy to undo. Before he could get his hand inside Mason's pants, Mason kissed a path down Falcon's body, tearing at his clothes as he went. Falcon should have felt guilt or nervousness. Instead, he felt like it wasn't him. Like the world had stopped turning and his life outside this room didn't exist. It was as if this wasn't happening at all. Falcon was free to enjoy the moment. As far as Falcon could tell, Mason hadn't told anyone about their last encounter. They were his secret, and he was safe with Mason—the last person he ever expected to want.

Then Falcon was nude. His cock was in Mason's mouth and nothing mattered any longer. He had lied about not remembering the last time. Mason had been right to accuse him of goading. He had known Mason's pride would demand he suck Falcon's dick again. Mason had one hell of a mouth. He knew how to use it. His tongue flicked Falcon's crown. His throat squeezed his length with perfection. Even the way his fingers probed at Falcon's ass was something Falcon expected he would want to stop. He didn't. Falcon massaged Mason's scalp as he fucked the man's mouth. His hips rotated as he tried for more. Everything was on fire. Falcon wondered if the heat exploding through him was the first sign of his life going up in flames. He begged for more with no shame.

A cry of denial rang from the walls as Mason crawled back up his body while pushing his jeans down his thighs. Before Falcon had time to lose his temper, or an ounce of heat, Mason's body covered Falcon. Their mouths clashed. Mason's dick rubbed against his in the most delicious way. Falcon found himself lifting his hips, trying for more. Mason's weight kept him pinned in place. The way Mason thrust against him had Falcon squirming. Pressure and pleasure combined to make him half insane with need. Falcon tore at Mason's skin with his short nails, trying to get closer. If Mason's tongue didn't fill Falcon's mouth, Falcon might have begged for release. As it was, he couldn't stop the whimpering noises in his throat. Mason's thrusts quickened. Falcon's body tensed. Under any other circumstances, Falcon might have considered this no more than a teenage make-out session. With Mason, it felt like making love, which fucked with Falcon a lot. The first spasm hit. A gasp stuck in Falcon's throat. His entire body convulsed as hot cum filled the space between their bodies. Mason tore his mouth away. The muscles in his neck stood out as he strained toward orgasm. Falcon couldn't close his eyes to the sight. A loud cry left Mason's lips. Falcon's body jerked in response. Mason's mouth covered Falcon's again, stealing everything from him —his air, Falcon's good sense, and more he couldn't admit. Fuck. Falcon didn't know what to do anymore. He was well past having gone too far.

THREE

MASON'S MIND was still on his empty bed, even as he wiped down the gym equipment as his final duty for the day. Falcon had been gone when Mason woke, and Mason couldn't let it go. He didn't know Falcon's number. There was no way for him to check on him. His pride stung at the thought, but he had driven by Incubus to see if Falcon's car was in the lot. It wasn't. Falcon must have called a cab. That was all Mason could think. No way had Falcon called Dillion to come rescue him from Mason's bed. Fuck. Mason didn't like himself today.

Falcon was Dillion's best friend. Mason hadn't let himself think too much about that last time. Maybe Dillion already hated Mason forever, but that changed nothing about the way Mason felt. He wasn't trying to hurt Dillion more. The first night he had spent with Falcon, Mason had been shitfaced. Last night, he hadn't had that excuse. Mason had been stone cold sober. Each move he had made had been intentional, making Mason wonder why he hadn't stopped. Dillion was his ex. Mason shouldn't care how he would feel if he ever found out. Mason knew Falcon couldn't say the same. This whole matter was a mess. Ex or not, Dillion was a great person. Mason couldn't let anything happen with Falcon again. It wasn't fair to anyone involved.

"If you need any help from a personal trainer, our lead trainer Mason is here to help."

At the sound of his name, Mason pasted on his most professional smile and turned. He still had an hour's worth of work to do and he needed this job. Falcon stood behind him, looking every bit as caustic as ever.

"Is there anywhere you don't work?"

Mason's co-worker David looked between them. "Oh, wow. Do you two already know each other?"

Falcon smirked. "Unfortunately."

"Oh dear," David muttered.

Mason couldn't let it go. "I see you're sober... for once." To his surprise, Falcon's smirk transformed into a genuine smile. His eyes danced with laughter. He looked like he was enjoying himself.

"Is this your second hunting ground?"

"My first, actually," Mason answered. Even he heard the laughter in his voice. David looked relieved. Not that Mason or Falcon paid him any attention. Their gazes barely wavered from each other. "I've worked here for fifteen years. Plus, I quit Incubus."

"Wow. Where will you find your twinks now?"

Mason shouldn't be enjoying this. He couldn't stop. "I'll stand still, and they'll come to me. After all, this is the third time I've stumbled over you."

A bark of laughter had heads turning their way and Falcon covering his mouth to stifle the sound.

Mason couldn't stop smiling.

David looked between them and cleared his throat. "Well, um. I'll be behind the counter if you need me."

Neither of them watched as David walked away.

"Seriously, though. What brings you by?" Another thought hit before Falcon had time to answer. "Where do you even live?"

"Vegas, but I travel a lot. A lot," he said again, stressing the words. "I'm in town pretty often and need a place to work out while I'm here. Do you get a lunch break?"

Mason blinked at the sudden change in topic. "I do, but I've already used it for the day, since I get off in an hour."

"Can I see you when you get off?"

"You were gone when I woke up." Fuck him. Mason had no clue where the words came from, but they sounded hurt, even to his ears. He tried to keep talking and move past his own needy statement. "Yes, you may see me when I get off." Goddamn. Hadn't he literally just told himself he wouldn't mess with Falcon again? He was a dumbass. Seeing him didn't equate sex. Spending time together was nothing. Friends did that all the time.

Falcon's mouth quirked. He looked like a total asshole and maybe he was, but so was Mason. "You should probably give me your number so we can figure something out." He dug out his phone as he made the claim. Mason rattled off his number while Falcon programmed him into his phone. "I sent you a text so you can save me too."

Since Falcon said the words to his phone, Mason couldn't get a read on him. Not that Mason ever had any idea what Falcon thought about anything. Falcon was always a complete surprise. "My phone is in my locker. I'll be sure to save your number when I leave."

Falcon's light blue gaze lifted. He met Mason's stare. "I had a shoot scheduled at seven this morning. That's why I was gone. I'll catch up with you later." With that promise hanging between them, Falcon walked away. Mason watched him go with no clue what just happened. Falcon wouldn't lose Dillion for him. Not only did Mason already know that, he didn't want to come between Dillion and Falcon. So what were they doing? Mason didn't know. All he knew was, no matter how many times he told himself to stop, draw a line, he didn't. He had no clue what was happening to his life, but Mason knew one thing with absolute certainty. This would end badly.

WAS HE WRONG? YES. FALCON FULLY ACCEPTED that reality as he waited for Mason to leave his fitness club. He kept trying to stop. When Falcon had slipped away from Mason's bed, he had told himself that was the end. By two hours later, Falcon still hadn't stopped thinking about him. Then he was looking in Mason's eyes again and asking to have more of his time. The thing was,

45

since Dillion started dating Beck, their friendship had taken a backseat. That was okay. Beck was supposed to come first, but Falcon didn't really have anyone else. Even though he spent a lot of time in Aspen, he didn't have any other friends here. He was always surrounded by people, but they were people who wanted something. Mason didn't even like him, much less want anything from Falcon. The man's distaste was oddly freeing. Even though he didn't like Falcon, Mason had still come to his rescue last night. No one else had stuck around to help. Falcon knew there was no real or good excuse for him to be here, but he couldn't leave. He was lonely, and he thought—maybe— Mason was too.

The black on black of Falcon's Hellcat made him nearly invisible to everyone outside of his car. That was why he didn't hide his smile as he caught sight of Mason stepping outside. His red hair was slicked back—like he was fresh from the shower. He had changed into jeans, and just like last night, they were baggy in the waist thanks to his massive thighs. His t-shirt protested his massive muscles. Several heads turned his way as he cut through the parking lot. Falcon tapped his horn. Mason's gaze moved his way. His mouth lifted in one corner and he changed directions. Falcon hit the button, rolling down the passenger-side window.

"Get in."

Mason glanced down at his gym bag, as if trying to decide what to do with it.

"Throw it in the back and get in."

Mason opened the back door and tossed the bag inside before crawling into the front seat. "Hey."

Falcon rolled the window back up and leaned Mason's way. "Hey," he said as he stole a kiss.

Mason didn't back down. In fact, he snagged Falcon's throat and deepened their kiss. Mason's strength was sexy as hell. Falcon was used to being in control. He knew he could take over anytime, but he liked it when Mason challenged him.

"That was unexpected," Mason said against his lips.

Falcon chuckled and felt Mason's lips stretch into a smile. Still, he didn't back away. He was sober. There was no excuse he could make this time. He had willingly waited for Mason for this. To have this. Mason pressed closer, half crawling into Falcon's seat to take control. It was like getting high. A wave of euphoria washed over him. Then a burst of laughter rang out as Mason found the button to lean back Falcon's seat. Mason's laughter mixed with his as he kept coming back for more kisses. The mood changed. Mason's tongue stroked his. Falcon's skin caught fire. His fingers found Mason's hair. He dragged Mason closer, giving back as much as he took. Falcon didn't doubt for a second they were steaming up the windows. His heart raced. Falcon didn't want to stop.

Mason pulled away and pressed his forehead to Falcon's. For a moment, they stared into each other's eyes. "You probably don't want to risk running into anyone with me. How do you feel about going to my place, ordering some food, and making out all night?"

Guilt struck from nowhere. Falcon floundered for a moment, wondering if he felt wrong for being with Mason or for making Mason feel like he was a secret. He was, but still. "Sounds great."

Mason brushed a light kiss across Falcon's lips. "Follow me home. I'll let you have my spot in the garage, so no one sees your car." He was so willing to let Falcon hide him. Too willing, in fact. Falcon wondered if he was the one being hidden. Damn, this was a mess. Not that Falcon was stopping.

"See you soon."

"Yep." Mason leapt from the car and Falcon fixed his seat to stop himself from watching him go. Nothing good would come of this. Funny how that thought became smaller with each passing moment. Falcon didn't want to sleep alone tonight. It seemed like everyone had someone, except Mason and him. All they had was each other, as fucked up as that might be.

———

MASON COULDN'T STOP CHECKING HIS MIRRORS to make sure Falcon didn't change his mind and ditch him. He couldn't recall the last time he felt so alive. Even while rearranging cars so Falcon could park in the garage, Mason questioned if he was dreaming. Falcon was sober. This wasn't some fluke. Falcon had willingly come to him.

He was a bit surprised to find Roman home. Usually, his roommate stayed gone on the weekends, having found a more than willing body to keep him busy until Roman got bored. Either he had gotten bored faster than usual or Roman was burned out on nameless faces. Either way, Mason knew he would have a bit of explaining to do the moment Roman set eyes on Falcon.

His hazel eyes moved from Falcon to Mason. Mason could practically feel the accusations swirling. "Hey." Roman swiped his hand on his jeans before holding it out to Falcon. "I'm Roman, Mason's roommate."

Falcon accepted his handshake. "Nice to meet you. I'm Falcon."

"I've seen your web show," Roman admitted. "You're... a bit terrifying actually."

Pride filled Mason's chest, even though he had no right to it. He had gotten his ass kicked by Falcon not that long ago. If anyone knew Falcon was way stronger than he appeared, it was Mason.

"Whatever you're cooking smells delicious," Falcon said, ignoring Roman's comment.

"Roman is always cooking."

Roman chuckled at Mason's words. "Or eating."

Falcon's gaze moved down Roman's body. "You don't look like it."

An unwanted spurt of jealousy hit Mason. Roman was gorgeous. He was tall, fit, and had impeccable hair. It was long, thick, and had the perfect amount of waviness. Roman was beautiful, and he knew it. After all, he was a stripper and his looks paid the rent.

Roman shrugged. "I dance all night, so I burn a lot of calories. Otherwise, you'd have to roll me out the house. I love food a little too much. Would you like to try my noodle-free lasagna?"

Falcon looked adorably confused. "How do you make lasagna without noodles?"

"With lots and lots of cheese," Roman said with a wink.

"I do love cheese."

Roman motioned Falcon toward the kitchen table. "Come eat, then. You're at the right house."

With a smile, Falcon moved to sit at the dining room table. Mason shook his head and followed. He had no idea what was happening to his life, but fuck it. Falcon was here and Mason would take it. His mind was still blown from last night. Even knowing it wouldn't take much more to leave him completely addicted, Mason couldn't stop. He needed something, anything to go right for him. Logically, he recognized everything about Falcon should feel wrong. It didn't. Mason couldn't stop until he knew why.

MASON'S GAZE FOLLOWED HIM EVERY SECOND OF the day. The constant staring should have been uncomfortable. Instead, Falcon felt powerful—like he controlled Mason with some invisible force Falcon hadn't realized he possessed before Mason.

Falcon was a man's man. He did guy stuff without apologies. Falcon fought professionally and for the hell of it. He drank, cursed, smoked pot and a cigar on occasion. Falcon stayed out late and went home with strangers. He had no plans to ever settle down. But no one, not one person, had ever shown him the power of his sexuality the way Mason did.

By the time Mason suggested they watch a movie in bed, Falcon was practically leaking in his jeans. He had been so fucking turned on since the moment he set eyes on Mason leaving the gym that Falcon thought his mind might snap. There was no way he could wait long enough to pretend they would watch a movie. The moment the door closed behind them, Falcon started stripping. Before Mason had time to register what would happen, Falcon hooked his foot and used the leverage to toss Mason onto the bed. A loud laugh rent the air. It turned into a moan when Falcon straddled Mason's body. He went straight for the neck, sucking and licking while undoing Mason's pants.

Mason squeezed his bare ass. "Goddamn. You're hot."

Falcon didn't give Mason time to cool. He stripped away the man's clothes, hearing something rip and uncaring. "Whatever that was, I'll replace it."

Falcon could afford to give Mason anything he wanted. In the heat of the moment, he would have given him anything he asked for. He kissed a path down Mason's body, stopping only long enough to lick Mason's cock, before diving for a stack of condoms and lube on the bedside table. Mason openly fought for air while Falcon suited up.

"You know," Mason said, sounding winded. "I'm usually on top."

Falcon squirted lube everywhere, barely hearing a word through the lust pressing in on him. "Not with me, you're not."

Without preamble, Falcon shoved Macon's knee higher and shoved his way inside. Mason cried out. Falcon froze at the sound. He breathed past the pleasure and prayed for strength. Falcon pressed his forehead to Mason's chest and sucked air. He refused to move until he felt Mason relax. Even then, he barely rocked. It wasn't his intention to hurt Mason. Falcon's usual patience was gone. He hadn't stopped thinking about the last time he had been inside Mason. He barely remembered that night, but occasionally images would slam into his mind, cramping his stomach with want. Falcon had never been so blown away by anyone.

Mason stroked his hair. At the sensation, Falcon

kissed Mason's chest. He changed angles and thrust. Mason moaned like he was already on edge. Falcon couldn't stop himself from lifting his chin and watching every changing nuance of Mason's expression. His cheeks were flushed. He looked half crazed. Falcon wanted him to come completely undone, so he palmed Mason's cock. Mason's stomach caved—like he couldn't take the ecstasy. His eyes looked wild. Falcon shifted his weight to his knees, positioning himself perfectly between Mason's thighs. He two-handed Mason's cock while sawing in and out of the man's ass. Mason gripped the comforter beneath him and held on. With his eyes squeezed shut and openly gasping, he fucked Falcon's hands. Falcon had no mercy. He tugged and squeezed, needing Mason's orgasm like he required oxygen to survive.

"You'll get down in the muck with me like you won't with anyone else, because it's me. Understood?"

Mason whimpered.

Falcon squeezed harder. "Understood? This ass is mine."

A cry bounced from the walls. Mason's entire body convulsed. His asshole clamped down on Falcon's dick before sucking him deeper. Jets of cum soaked Mason's torso. He shamelessly writhed in Falcon's hands. Falcon didn't stop pumping, purposely tormenting Mason even as the man's body sucked him dry and his mind flew apart. Falcon had never experienced anything more powerful with anyone. He was scared as hell he would never be able to walk away.

FOUR

THE BED WAS EMPTY. Falcon checked the time. It was almost nine in the morning. Damn. It was too early for Falcon's blood. He was used to staying up all night and sleeping all day. Instead, he had gone to bed at a decent time—like an old man. Except he had fucked like a teenager all night. He fought a smile at the thought.

After finding his stuff, Falcon ran through his usual morning routine. When he came out of the bathroom, he heard the faint vibration of an incoming text. His phone crawled across Mason's nightstand. Falcon snagged it and checked his messages.

Dillion: *Are you still coming to town sometime this week?*

Falcon: *I'm on my way.*

Dillion: *Don't text and drive. I'll see you when you get here. Love you.*

Guilt fell like a hammer. Dillion was the most important person in his life. Being here would ruin everything. His phone buzzed again.

Dillion: *Just a heads up. Beck and I might not be here the whole time you're in town. We have a beach trip planned later in the week, but even after we're gone, you're still more than welcome to crash at our place. You know it's your home too.*

A pit of loneliness opened inside Falcon. He was no longer the most important person in Dillion's life. Dillion didn't make trips to see him anymore. In truth, he barely spent any time with Falcon at all. Not that Falcon blamed him. He would be someone else's husband soon. Dillion's first responsibility was to Beck now. Falcon was just kind of in the way.

He took a deep breath and set his phone aside. The scent of brewing coffee overcame him. Falcon followed the smell and found Roman eating cereal while standing over the sink. His hair was up in a messy bun and he wore only leggings. He gave Falcon a fat-cheeked smile with his mouth stuffed full of cereal.

"Want some?" Roman asked around his huge bite.

Falcon shook his head. "Where did Mason go?"

Roman nodded toward the hall and swallowed. "Third door on the left."

Falcon headed back down the hall, following Roman's instructions. He found Mason sitting in a leather chair with a deep line furrowed in his brow as he glared at a knot of yellow yarn and tugged. He glanced up as Falcon cleared the door. His expression cleared as his cheeks turned red. "Oh. Hey. I didn't know you were awake." He tried shoving the yarn into a bag, but it was too late.

Falcon crossed the room, plopped down in Mason's lap so he couldn't get away, and snagged the canvas bag. "What are you doing in here?" He peered inside while pushing away Mason's hands when he tried snatching the bag away. Yarn and knitting needles along with patterns filled the sack.

Mason huffed.

Falcon looked from the contents to Mason's blushing face. "Do you knit?"

"It's no big deal," Mason said, plucking the bag from Falcon and setting it aside. He kept his gaze averted. "It's just something my mom taught me, and then I met Dillion's dad. You know, he's the chief of staff at the hospital. He mentioned they were always needing preemie hats and I have nothing but time, so you know..." He rubbed the back of his neck, looking two steps beyond horrified.

"You knit hats for the preemies." Falcon repeated the words because he couldn't believe what he was hearing. This gigantic man, who was an asshole more often than not, made hats to donate to babies. "That's adorable."

Mason's gaze slid away. "Okay. You don't have to make fun of me."

Falcon shook his head. "I'm not. That's a really nice thing to do. I'm just surprised. You're not that nice."

"Thanks." Damn. Mason sounded tired.

With no real plan, Falcon shifted positions and straddled Mason's lap. His fingers found the ends of Mason's hair and twirled. "I'm not complaining." Falcon moved closer and nipped at Mason's bottom lip. "I like that you can surprise me. Not much does." He pushed away. "I guess I'd better get going. You've got preemie hats to make, and I should do... something."

Mason moved as if to stand. Instead, he snagged Falcon around the waist and hauled him forward. He pressed his lips to Falcon's stomach. For a moment, Mason stayed like that. The move punched Falcon in the chest for some reason he couldn't explain. Then, Mason came to his feet, and the moment was over. "I'd ask you to tell Dillion hi from me, but you know, then you'd have to tell on yourself."

Oh, good. The asshole was back. Falcon didn't feel off kilter with this version of Mason.

Falcon winked. "Maybe I'll tell him I ran into his dad, and he told me you knit, so we can joke about how you used to tell him people would laugh at him for wearing women's clothes."

"It must be nice to be you."

Mason's words confused the hell of Falcon, especially when he didn't expound. Falcon questioned if that was the point.

IT MUST BE NICE TO BE YOU. DAMN. MASON needed to do a better job of hiding his heart from Falcon. Otherwise, Falcon would crush him. Of course, Mason had probably seen the last of Falcon. They weren't a couple. He was a way Falcon passed the time. In fact, it hadn't escaped Mason that it was possible Falcon was getting a bit of revenge against him for all the hell Mason put Dillion through. The ax could still fall. Falcon bringing up Mason's transgressions against Dillion wearing women's clothing gave credence to that thought. Mason had made a lot of mistakes with Dillion. Ninety-nine percent of those errors had everything to do with Dillion's age. The other one percent was Dillion's fame. Here, in Aspen, where tons of celebrities lived as regular people, Dillion felt safe. Sometimes, Mason thought Dillion felt a little too safe and that confidence would get him hurt. Not everyone was as accepting as the town he lived in. If he wouldn't go out with security, then he needed to think about how he went out dressed.

Mason closed his mind against those thoughts. Dillion wasn't his concern anymore. Mason had his time in the sun with Dillion and with Falcon. Neither man should have looked his way. There was nothing special about Mason. Sometimes, that was a hard pill to swallow. He wanted to believe he was good enough to win people like them—men everyone dreamed to have. Mason liked the idea of making everyone jealous. He realized that was his pride talking.

Roman poked his head in the room. "Now that Falcon's gone, I have questions."

A sardonic smile touched Mason's lips. "Yeah. Me too."

"Isn't that dude your ex's best friend?"

"Yep." Even Mason heard the horror in his answer.

Roman blinked. "All right." He dragged out the words, sounding confused. Roman wasn't alone.

"I didn't seek him out." Mason needed Roman to know he wasn't a complete piece of shit. "It just kind of happened."

Roman pulled his hair from its bun and smoothed it out before pulling it up again. "You're a grown man. I'm sure you know what you're doing."

Mason thought that was giving him way too much credit, but whatever. "I doubt he'll come around again. It really was just one of those things."

"If you say so." Roman didn't sound convinced. Probably because Mason didn't either. He didn't want to like Falcon, but he kind of did. Mason wouldn't admit it aloud. Falcon would never care about him, so it was pointless to feel anything at all.

With a sigh, Mason kicked his feet up and grabbed his knitting. Fuck everything. He was getting old anyhow. Mason might as well get some hats done.

Falcon: *It occurs to me, with all these damn windows in Dillion's house, it must've been super easy for you to thoroughly stalk him.*

Mason: *Wow. I was never that bad.*

Falcon: *Are you saying you don't like to watch?*

Mason: *I much rather participate. I'm not a sidelines kind of guy.*

Falcon: *I can see that. I'm surprised you're still awake.*

Mason: *It seems I'm still on Incubus time. I'm not used to going to bed before four in the morning. What's your excuse?*

Falcon: *I'm not eighty.*

Falcon: *I wasn't trying to insult you. As much as it probably seems like I'm always trying to be an ass, I wasn't this time.*

Mason: *Okay.*

Mason: *I'll be up for a while, if you get bored.*

Falcon: *Can I call?*

Mason: *Anytime you want.*

Falcon smiled at his phone. There was no one there to see him and judge him. He was free to steal a small moment of guilt-free happiness. Falcon felt a bit like an idiot, but he hadn't stopped thinking about

Mason all day. He stared out the large window inside his assigned bedroom at Dillion's. This was his room. Falcon had clothes that stayed here. No one else ever used this room. It was his. Falcon's chest tightened. That was how close he was to Dillion. They were each other's chosen family. He should leave Mason alone. The phone rang in his hand. Falcon looked down and spotted Mason's name flashing across the face of his phone. He couldn't stop himself from pressing the device to his ear.

"Hey."

"I couldn't take the strain of waiting to see if you would call me. So I called first."

Falcon swiped his fingers across his mouth, trying to physically wipe away his smile. It didn't work. He pressed his forehead against the window and stared at the surrounding trees, trying to cool his skin. "What did you do with the rest of your day?"

"Nothing."

"Literally nothing, huh?"

Mason laughed. It was low and sexy-sounding. Falcon swore he could feel it against his skin. "Not literally nothing. I moved occasionally, breathed, ate, and had a lot of thoughts."

Falcon couldn't stop smiling. His cheeks ached. "Were any of those thoughts worth sharing?"

"I've decided I don't dislike you."

A burst of laughter escaped Falcon at the confession. "Sounds like I'm not trying hard enough."

"Who's not hard enough?" Mason asked the question fast and mumbled—like he was hard of hearing.

Falcon's body shook with silent laughter. He blew out a sigh. "Take me to bed."

"Gladly, but you're not here," Mason said without skipping a beat.

"I meant the phone. Take me to bed."

Something brushed across the phone and a moment passed before Mason responded. "All right. In bed."

"Close your eyes and breathe."

"Okay." Mason sounded confused.

"Hush and listen." When Mason didn't respond, Falcon smiled. At least Mason could follow orders. "Breathe deep." He heard Mason take a breath. "Concentrate on your right foot. Let it relax. Once the muscles are completely relaxed, move to the left. Eventually, the rest of your body will follow. Don't get up. I want you to go to sleep. Goodnight, sexy."

"Goodnight."

Falcon disconnected their call and went back to

staring out the window. He wondered if Mason would actually sleep. Falcon rubbed his chest. There was something wrong with Falcon's breathing. He should go home and distance himself from this. That was the smart thing to do. The right thing. But was it the best thing for him? Falcon no longer knew. Things didn't feel quite so black and white anymore. Falcon kind of wanted to be with Mason. Damn.

FALCON: *I WAS LOADING UP MY CAR, GETTING ready to head home, and I noticed your gym bag is still in my backseat.*

Mason: *Damn. Do you want to meet somewhere so I can get it back?*

Falcon: *I can bring it to you. Are you home?*

Mason: *Yeah.*

Falcon: *I'll be there in thirty. Is that okay?*

Mason: *See you then.*

For longer than he cared to admit, Mason had lain awake, thinking about Falcon. Now he couldn't stop looking out the window and watching for his arrival. When Falcon pulled into the driveway, Mason leapt from the couch and headed out to meet him. He beat back the thought that he looked a little too excited. Mason measured his steps, hoping he wouldn't look like he had rushed out there to meet Falcon, exactly like he had.

Falcon stepped out from the car with Mason's bag in hand. "Hey."

"Hey." Even Mason heard the happiness in his voice. He relieved Falcon of the bag. "Thanks for this. I totally forgot about tossing it in your backseat."

"It's no big deal." Falcon shifted from one foot to the other. His gaze never wavered from Mason. "So, how did you sleep?"

"Like the dead," Mason lied with zero shame. After all, no one had ever tried helping him fall sleep before. Mason wouldn't let Falcon's efforts look wasted. "What about you?"

Falcon shrugged. "Good enough, I guess."

Mason hugged the bag to his chest. "So... you're headed home?"

Falcon nodded. "Dillion and Beck left for Cancun this morning. There's no sense in me hanging around their house while they're away." He shifted again, looking uncomfortable. Mason wondered if he didn't really want to leave.

"You could always stay a little while longer... with me." Mason didn't really think things through. He doubted Falcon would be any more willing to hang around his house, while Mason worked, than he had been willing to hang around Dillion's. After all, Dillion had an indoor pool and shit. Mason had nothing to offer but himself. That wasn't much incentive.

Falcon's mouth twitched like he fought a smile. "Was that an invitation?"

It was hard, but Mason managed to stand still. The desire to shift nervously was real. "Yes." Goddamn, Falcon was wickedly beautiful. His expression screamed Mason would get dicked down if Falcon decided to stay. "What's my incentive?" Falcon shifted closer. His hand slid across Mason's hip.

Mason chose honesty. "Just me. You'll probably get bored."

"I'm not as sure."

An unfamiliar pressure grew in Mason's chest. "Is that a yes?"

Falcon's eyes flashed with humor. "Kiss me and convince me."

Without a qualm, Mason tossed his bag aside and pulled Falcon against him. He liked the way Falcon fit in his arms. Falcon was the perfect size. He lowered his head. Falcon met him halfway. When their lips met, neither of them immediately moved to deepen the kiss. They shared air. Then, Falcon's teeth sank into Mason's bottom lip. Mason lost his breath.

"Stay," Mason begged against Falcon's lips.

Falcon buried his fingers in Mason's hair and pulled him even closer. "Make me leave."

No. Mason couldn't do it. He was more likely to plead with Falcon to stay for good. "Stay," he repeated instead.

Falcon gave a faint nod. Mason felt the answer to his soul. He hadn't lost Falcon yet. Temporary reprieve or not, Mason wanted every second he could get. He would make the best of his time. It wasn't like he had expected any of this. Mason knew a lucky break when he saw one.

FIVE

HE HAD BEEN COMING to Mason's work for over a month, stealing time with Mason while he worked. Occasionally, Falcon would stay a couple of nights at Dillion's, because he was in town. Twice, he flew out of state for fights. Both times, he had come straight back to Aspen the same night. He needed to go home. Staying here was pushing his luck. Each time Falcon thought to leave, Mason asked him to stay. Falcon always caved, even though he had no idea why.

Falcon was happy. That was the oddest part of the entire fucked-up mess. For the first time in his life, he was properly rested and fed. It was like he had always needed a keeper. He just hadn't realized it until Mason had taken the job. Still, Falcon refused to think of them as a couple. He hadn't demanded Mason be faithful to only him, even though they didn't give each other time for anyone else. Falcon refused to think of them as anything at all. Any title meant he had betrayed his best friend beyond the point of forgiveness. Falcon couldn't live with that.

The small gym where Mason worked was dead. At eleven o'clock on a Thursday night, no one worked out, it seemed. Mason still had an hour left on the clock, but he was getting his own workout in, since there was nothing else to do. Falcon couldn't stop watching. Mason was sexy as hell. There wasn't a single part of him that wasn't perfect. It was fascinating to watch his muscles move and flex with every exercise. When he dropped to the mat for sit-ups, Falcon didn't pass up the opportunity. He straddled Mason's hips.

Mason didn't move. Instead, he massaged Falcon's hips, rocking him forward and trying to seduce him.

Falcon wasn't having it. He wasn't finished watching. "Come on," he said, poking Mason in his rock-hard abs. "You didn't get this body by being lazy. Show me what you've got."

Mason linked his fingers behind his head and

lifted just enough to deepen the lines in his cut stomach. His smile screamed wicked intent. "What will you give me if I do?"

They were alone. The place was completely devoid of life. No one could see. "A kiss, but," he said, dragging out the word, "you have to come get it."

Mason rolled upward in a show of strength that was hot as fuck. He pressed a quick kiss to Falcon's lips before Falcon could get away. His laughter filled the gym as he kept coming back for more. With every sit-up, Mason stole another kiss until Falcon snagged the back of his neck and refused to let him get away. Mason's laughter died as their tongues met. Something that had been stirring in Falcon's chest grew. He held Mason's face between his hands, stroking the man's cheeks with his thumbs. Falcon didn't want to move, but they couldn't stay like this all night.

"Do you get vacation time here?"

Mason blinked, as if coming back to himself. "Yeah."

Falcon brushed another light kiss across Mason's lips. "Come stay with me."

Mason blinked some more, looking lost. "I'm sorry."

Falcon nodded as the idea grew larger inside his head. "I say you need a vacation, and I live in one of the biggest tourist spots around. Come stay with me. I'll show you a good time," Falcon said with a wink.

He could see the hope growing in Mason's eyes, but he didn't immediately agree. "As thrilled as I am at the idea of having you to myself without any interruptions, what happens when Dillion finds out about me?"

Falcon's smile slipped away. He felt it melt away. It was almost funny how much he hated the sound of Dillion's name on Mason's lips. He knew they should have talked about this already. In truth, he couldn't believe Mason had made it this long without asking. It seemed there was no avoiding it any longer. "He won't."

"And if he does?"

Falcon had to be honest—with Mason and himself. "Then we're over."

Mason's gaze immediately skirted away, hiding his heart. He cleared his throat. It was an uncomfortable sound.

Falcon rushed to fix things. He wouldn't let Dillion find out about them, not only because he couldn't lose Dillion, but because Falcon recognized he also didn't want to lose Mason. Like it or not, he cared. Falcon invaded Mason's space even further. He touched Mason's chin and urged Mason to meet his stare. When he did, Falcon could see his heart in his eyes. Falcon couldn't look away. "Come stay with me. Vegas is over six hundred miles away. No one will know you're there. You can ride home with me. When you're ready to come home, I'll buy you a plane ticket. You can enjoy some time off. I get to spend some quality time with you. Everyone wins. Please?"

Mason took a deep breath. His chest expanded, fascinating Falcon. "Okay."

It felt like a win. Falcon couldn't suppress the smile that exploded across his face. Soon, he would have Mason all to himself with no fear of getting caught. He would spoil the fuck out of Mason, and then—who knew—maybe they could figure out a way to make this work long term. Falcon didn't have the slightest fucking clue how that was possible. Hope was all he had. For now, he would cling to it. Falcon wasn't ready to go back to being lonely. He wasn't ready to lose Mason.

SIX

FALCON'S HOUSE was something out of a dream. His pool alone made Mason glad they had dated a while before Mason saw the place. While he had always known Falcon was out of his league, Falcon's house was insane. Mason wanted to move into Falcon's pool house and become the man's sex slave, even if Falcon wanted nothing more from him. The bed inside the pool house was amazing. Soft yet firm enough to take the abuse they had been giving it all day.

"What are you thinking about, gorgeous?"

Mason snuggled closer to Falcon's touch. He loved the way Falcon massaged his scalp. "Mmmm. I'm wondering where I need to put in my application to be your daddy. I mean, like I don't have any money or anything to offer, but I'd be your whipping daddy. You could put a leash on me, and I'd follow you anywhere."

Falcon's whole body shook with laughter. With Mason draped over him like a blanket, and their bodies stuck together with their sweat, Mason was in heaven. He loved the way Falcon felt beneath him. Mason pressed his ear against Falcon's chest, hunting for the sound of Falcon's laughter.

"I'd say you've had your application in for a while. You should at least get an interview."

"I should say," Mason agreed.

"Hmmm." The hum coming from Falcon's throat was so sexy, Mason found himself licking the man's neck and trying to taste it. Falcon rubbed his back. "What do you consider your greatest strength?"

Mason didn't hesitate. "Sucking dick."

"Agreed." Mason loved the way Falcon didn't miss a beat. "What's your biggest weakness?"

"This sexy body," Mason said, crawling higher and stealing a quick kiss while feeling Falcon up. "I can't get enough. It's all I think about. I'd go as far as to say it hinders my other work."

Falcon's laughter made everything worthwhile. "Where do you see yourself in five years?"

Mason dropped his head and went back to

licking Falcon's neck to hide his immediate reaction. There was no way his face didn't show his gut-wrenching desire to keep Falcon. He kept his tone light. "Right here, slaving away for you."

Falcon turned breathless as Mason worked harder at seducing the man—like he hadn't just had him. "If you could have any job in the world, no matter how far-fetched, what would it be?"

"This, of course."

Falcon tugged his hair, leaving Mason no other choice but to lift his head and meet Falcon's stare. He looked serious and unmoving. "For real, if you could have anything you wanted, no limits, what would it be?"

You. The thought hit so hard; Mason didn't know how Falcon didn't hear it. "I guess I wish I could be debt free so I wouldn't have to worry so much all the time." As the lie rolled from his tongue, Mason felt his self-hatred grow. For the first time in his life, Mason knew exactly what he wanted, and he couldn't be honest.

Using his skills against Mason, the way Falcon liked to do, he flipped, rolling Mason beneath him. With his chin resting on his stacked hands, Falcon stared at Mason from his spot perched on Mason's chest. "Who else have you applied with?"

A chuckle escaped Mason. Falcon looked so serious while asking the most random questions. "No one. You're the only one I'm interested in working with at this time."

"What sort of salary do you expect?"

Mason pretended to think it over. This was the most extensive interview he had ever endured, especially for a fake job. "All your kisses, of course. Definitely your exclusivity. As much of your time as you're willing to give." Mason gave him a short nod. "Basically, as much of you as I can get."

"Do I get your exclusivity in this arrangement?"

Mason wondered if Falcon was blind. "You've always had it."

Falcon dropped a kiss to the center of Mason's chest. "Well, I have to say, you're one of my top candidates for the job."

Mason smiled to hide the way the remark cut. "Good to know I'm in the top ten or whatever." The way Falcon's expression shifted slightly let Mason know he wasn't hiding his feelings as well as he would like. He tried changing the subject. "What's on the agenda for tomorrow?"

Falcon shimmied lower. He kissed Mason's sternum. His gaze turned heated. He moved even lower and pressed his lips to Mason's stomach.

Mason found himself lifting his head to keep an eye on Falcon. He didn't want to miss a thing. "You know you're the only person I'm dating, right?" Falcon's question caught Mason off guard. He was so fixated on what Falcon was doing, it took him a moment to register his words.

"I didn't know, but I'm glad." Even to Mason's ears, he sounded breathless.

Falcon lowered his head. While holding Mason's stare, he circled Mason's navel with his tongue. He was so close to where Mason really wanted him. Mason could feel Falcon's every breath brushing his erection. "You keep me busy."

"I tr—" The words died on a gasp as Falcon sucked the tip of Mason's cock into his mouth. Just the head. Hard. Mason dropped his head and sucked air. Falcon made his head spin. Mason didn't know how much of this he could survive. Sometimes he felt like, since the day they first gave in to temptation, Falcon had kept him glued to the bed. He had never been in a relationship with anyone who had so much stamina, or such a huge appetite. Mason was damn near twice Falcon's age. He might live through this. If not, at least he would die a happy man.

THE UNHAPPINESS IN MASON'S EYES NEEDED TO disappear. Falcon couldn't breathe. He didn't know why he couldn't give an inch and let Mason see at least a little of his heart. That wasn't true. Falcon knew exactly why he kept his heart hidden. No matter how right Mason felt in every fucking way, he would always be wrong for Falcon in the way it mattered most—Dillion. Falcon hated everything about this, except for every second he spent with Mason. When they were together, it didn't feel wrong. In fact, Falcon was pretty sure Mason was the other half of his soul. This was such a fucked-up mess.

Falcon was so desperate to keep Mason; he was thinking seriously about asking Mason to move in with him. Mason would have to leave his house and job. That was a lot to ask when Falcon was offering none of himself in return. He wasn't willing to sacrifice a goddamn thing for Mason. Yet, he wished Mason would give up everything for him. Falcon knew he was a shitty person. He had always known that. Still, he couldn't stop wishing and wanting. Mason had no idea how unique he was to Falcon. If he did, he would never look at Falcon like he had moments ago—like Mason knew he would never be special to Falcon. He already was extraordinary.

Salty pre-cum leaked onto Falcon's tongue. Falcon couldn't stop searching for more. He had always loved salty things. Sucking Mason's dick was empowering as hell. He owned Mason in every way in that moment. Falcon could do anything. The problem was, he was held every bit as captive. If Mason knew how much power he wielded over Falcon, Falcon would be terrified. He already was to an extent. Falcon lived in constant fear of losing Mason. It was stupid and reckless, but fuck him, he cared.

Mason moaned. The sound punched Falcon in the gut, sounding like it came from Mason's soul. Falcon doubled his effects, sucking only the head of Mason's cock. He knew Mason. Falcon had watched and studied. Mason had the most sensitive crown. Anytime Falcon brushed the head of Mason's cock, Mason nearly came unglued. Falcon used the knowledge to torment him now. Mason shook and gasped beneath him, straining toward orgasm. Falcon was so tuned in to Mason's pleasure, he barely noticed his own needs at all. This was servicing Falcon's greatest desire—pleasing Mason. The man was a secret sickness. He would level Falcon's life, eventually. There was no escaping that fate.

As Mason cried out and cum filled Falcon's

mouth, an odd wave of sadness overcame Falcon. It swept over him from nowhere—like it had always been there, waiting for his guard to drop. Falcon recognized he was cramming as many experiences as he could into every second he spent with Mason because their time was short. The clock ticked down in Falcon's head. Soon, they would be over. Falcon wanted as many memories as he could get, because if he knew nothing else, Falcon knew he would lose Mason in the end. The knowledge hurt. Falcon couldn't even imagine what the real moment would be like. He wondered if he would survive.

THE INCESSANT RINGING WOULDN'T STOP. Mason was so fucking tired. It seemed like he had just fallen asleep. He tried covering his ears with his pillow, but it wouldn't shut out the sound. The ringing stopped before immediately starting again.

"For the love of all things holy, make it stop."

Falcon finally snatched up the phone. "Hello?" He immediately sat up, putting Mason on high alert. Mason was awake now. Falcon pushed the covers aside and stood. "I'm on my way."

Mason watched and waited. Their time was over

already. He felt it. He shouldn't have wasted his vacation time and savings, paying off his bills a month in advance so he could come here. He had felt in his gut it was a bad idea.

"Let me look at flights. It might be quicker if I drive." Falcon rubbed his forehead. "Damn. That would take like ten hours. Let me see which way would get me there the quickest and I'll be there. Okay? Just hang on."

Worry ate at Mason's gut. There was obviously something going on with Dillion. He could see the panic in Falcon's eyes. There was no one else who could move Falcon but Dillion. Falcon sat. Hard. Like his knees gave out. Mason immediately moved to offer what comfort he could. He pressed his lips to Falcon's shoulder. "I'm on my way. I promise, baby."

Even once Falcon disconnected the call, he didn't look Mason's way. He pulled up a flight app on his phone and started scrolling. Mason broke. "Is everything okay?"

At the question, Falcon twisted and looked behind him. "I don't know." He took an audible breath, as if trying to decide what to say. "It's... Sorry. I have to go to Aspen."

A sardonic smile tugged at Mason's lips. Falcon always acted like he couldn't say Dillion's name in his presence. "You can say his name, you know? I won't start foaming at the mouth with unrequited desire."

The guilt in Falcon's expression was real. He didn't have to say anything. It was written all over Falcon's face. Mason had hit the nail on the head. "I know you're supposed to be here for a while. If you want, you can fly back with me."

Mason dropped his gaze to his lap, hiding his feelings the way he always did with Falcon. If he knew nothing else, he knew feeling anything at all would drive Falcon away. "No. I think I'll stay. Surely there's a cheap hotel room nearby. I might as well enjoy my vacation." Because fuck it. He had known all along he wasn't important.

Falcon shifted to his knees and straddled Mason's lap, knocking him onto his back. "Stay here. No matter what, I'll be back by Tuesday. Okay?"

Hope flared in Mason's chest. He didn't want to believe in the affection he saw in Falcon's expression, but hope was a crazy thing. "Okay. Don't you need to go?" Even as Mason posed the question, he massaged Falcon's ass between his hands. He didn't want Falcon to rush off, but he knew how much Dillion meant to him.

"Not yet. I have a couple of hours to waste with

you. Let's make it count." He kissed Mason's chin.

As much as Mason wanted the erection that had sprung between them and was digging into Mason's hip, he also wanted to know why he was being abandoned. "Falcon." Even Mason heard the breathless note to his voice. "What's going on?"

"I'm seducing you." Falcon slid lower and kissed Mason's neck, lending power to his words. Mason was already hard.

"Agreed, but what's happened with Dillion?"

Falcon moved even lower. His teeth scraped Mason's nipple. "Beck is in the hospital." Mason sucked in a gasp as Falcon palmed his erection. "I'll be back as fast as I can. You won't have time to miss me."

"Awful cheeky of you to assume I'll miss you."

Falcon chuckled against his skin.

Falcon moved higher and sucked Mason's neck. Mason's breath came out in a pant as Falcon rocked against him. He urged Mason's knee higher. His erection probed at Mason's ass, making Mason gasp for air. Mason's entire body became one huge nerve ending, completely focused on Falcon's touch. "Admit you'll miss me," Falcon whispered against his neck. "Tell me you'll see me everywhere you look and wish I was here."

Mason's mind was a mess. He didn't know how he had let Falcon get under his skin. It wasn't fair for him to always fall for people so far out of his league, he could never truly have them. "You're already too sure of yourself. If I tell you I'll miss you, you'll be sure to crush me."

Falcon went still. Mason nearly cried out in denial and longing. His skin was on fire. Falcon was the only one who could fix him. Falcon leaned away and stared down at Mason. The vulnerability written on Falcon's face froze the air in Mason's lungs. He couldn't let himself hope. Falcon really would destroy him one day, probably sooner rather than later. Falcon slowly lowered his head. His eyes fell closed as he came in for a kiss. Mason never looked away. He wanted to memorize every second. Half a breath before Falcon's lips touched Mason's, he whispered, "I'll miss you."

Mason's heart squeezed in his chest at Falcon's confession. He was so royally fucked. He would do anything, give anything, if he could keep Falcon. But everything between them ended at one detail that would never change, Falcon would never choose Mason over Dillion, and Dillion would never forgive Falcon for this.

SEVEN

DILLION WAS A COMPLETE WRECK. The way he had sounded on the phone didn't touch the real thing. His eyes were bloodshot, and his nose was red. Dillion's face was splotchy. He looked like hell. Falcon tried several times to convince him to stop pacing. The wild look in Dillion's eyes had Falcon letting it go.

By the time the surgeon came out to talk to Dillion, Falcon wondered if he would be the one to collapse beneath Dillion's strain.

Dillion rushed the surgeon. "How is he?" Falcon moved to join him, ready for anything at this point.

The man's dark blue gaze moved between them. He didn't look like a man ready to drop bad news. That was good. "He's sleeping off the anesthesia right now. His appendix ruptured and made a mess. Usually, if we catch appendicitis in time, we can do surgery using a laser, which is minimally invasive. Unfortunately, that didn't happen in this case. So he has a pretty big incision, but I feel good that we got all the infection cleaned away. He'll need to stay a couple of days to be on the safe side. We don't like to take chances in cases like this."

"Of course." Dillion nodded, obviously willing to do whatever it took to keep Beck healthy. "How long before I can see him?"

"He'll stay in recovery about another hour, and then they'll take him to his room. If you want to grab something to eat or run home to gather your things for a few days' stay, now would be a good time."

Dillion didn't stop nodding. "Okay. Thank you. Seriously. I appreciate everything."

Unexpectedly, the man took Dillion's hand and held it between his. "He'll be okay. Don't worry."

Since Falcon was about ninety percent sure Dillion was about to start crying again, he thanked the doctor and steered Dillion away. With Dillion's father being the chief of staff, and Dillion being two steps beyond famous, they'd given him a private waiting room and seen to his every need. Still, Falcon got the feeling Dillion wouldn't stop crying and climbing the walls until he set eyes on Beck. "What do you need, sweetie? Do you need me to get you something to eat or drive you home? I don't want to leave you alone, but if you rather I go pack you an overnight bag, I will."

Dillion growled. Despite the situation, the sound made Falcon smile. "I don't know. I can't make a decision right now. My brain is too bogged down."

That was all Falcon needed to hear to take charge. "All right. Let's go. We'll run through a drive-thru and grab you something to go. You have to keep your strength up so you can be there for Beck. Then we'll run to the house and grab your stuff. We'll be back before Beck gets to his room." Being in charge was Falcon's strong suit. He felt better the moment he took control. Beck would be fine. Dillion would too. And Falcon would be back with Mason by Tuesday, as promised. Everything would work out just fine.

MASON WAS DOING HIS DAMNEDEST NOT TO climb the walls. It wasn't that he cared about Dillion, except he kind of cared about Dillion. He didn't want anything bad to happen to the guy. Also,

Mason recognized if anything happened to Falcon, Mason would be devastated. Yeah, he completely realized he was comparing his relationship with Falcon the one Dillion had with Beck, but screw it. No one could hear his thoughts and judge him. He was in love with Falcon. Was it dumb? Fuck yeah, it was. This ended one way—with Mason licking his wounds. Just like with everything in his life, Mason had zero control. He felt how he felt. There was no sense in lying.

The phone rang in his hand, scaring the hell out of Mason. His heart raced into his throat as he rushed to answer.

"Hello?"

"What are you wearing?"

A relieved chuckle escaped Mason at Falcon's sultry tone. "Board shorts with black dress socks and sandals. My shirt has a hole in it right near my navel."

Falcon's laughter made his ridiculousness worthwhile. "I wish I was there to see it."

"Anytime you need to feed your geriatric fetish, I'm here for you."

Another sexy chuckle rumbled across Mason's ear. "I miss you already."

Mason drew a slow breath through his nose at

the confession. They were headed somewhere. He didn't want to hope. "I miss you too. How's Beck?"

"He's okay. At first, they said he would have to stay a few days in the hospital. He's done much better than they expected, so he might get to come home early. I'm ready to be back home with you."

"You're needed there."

"I know." Falcon sounded so sad.

Mason couldn't take it. "You're needed here too."

"Is that so?" Mason loved the way Falcon transformed, turning sexual in an instant. "Tell me how I can assist you, Mr. Jacobs."

Mason moved to stare out the French doors, leading out to the pool. The moonlight glimmered off the water. Despite Falcon's willingness to play, he sounded exhausted. It was Mason's job to take care of him. "You can take me to bed."

"Already there."

"Good boy," Mason praised. "Now close your eyes and breathe deep."

Falcon chuckled, obviously realizing Mason was trying to put him to sleep the same way Falcon had done for him the first time they had talked on the phone. "Should I concentrate on my right foot?"

Mason fought a smile. "How did you know?"

"Lucky guess. What are you doing right now, baby?"

"Staring at the pool. Wishing you were here."

"Maybe we should both go to bed? That way, we'll be one day closer to me coming home."

Mason rubbed his chest. He didn't feel better. For some reason he couldn't explain, the closer he got to Falcon coming home, the shorter their time together felt. "That sounds like a good plan."

"I'll see you soon, sexy."

"Okay. Goodnight, gorgeous."

"Goodnight."

Mason dropped his arm and pressed the phone to his chest. He swore it felt like he had already lost Falcon, and he didn't know why. Maybe he was just so used to nothing good ever lasting for him, that he didn't know how to accept this. Or maybe Mason just knew they were on their last breath.

GETTING BECK SETTLED AT HOME WAS HARDER work than Falcon anticipated. First there had been the slow drive from the hospital while Falcon did his best not to jar Beck too much. Then, after getting Beck settled on the couch, Dillion handed Beck the

TV remote and his cellphone while they headed right back out to get his meds. Beck looked tired and miserable, but the poor guy still worried more about Dillion than himself. They were adorable. Dillion fussed over Beck while Beck repeatedly asked Dillion if he was okay. Falcon was ready to go home.

He fixed Dillion some hot tea while plotting the best way to head back to Vegas with minimal fuss. Dillion ended up being the one to broach the topic.

"I'm sure you'll be glad to be back in your own bed," Dillion said as Falcon set the cup in front of him.

"Yes." He didn't see the point in lying. "I mean, if you need me to stay, I will, but I have a match in two days and things to put in order."

Dillion flashed him a tired-looking smile. "No. Don't worry over me. I can't tell you how much I appreciate you coming to the rescue." He rubbed his forehead. "I've never been so scared in all my days. It'll probably take me a while to get over it," Dillion added with a chuckle. "But having you here has been a major he—" Dillion froze mid-speech and tilted his head as if listening. Familiar music filled the air. "Ugh. Beck must've fallen asleep with the TV on. There's no way he would willingly choose to watch that awful gossipy TV show." Dillion moved to the living room. Falcon followed on his heels. While Dillion hunted for the remote, Falcon sneaked a peek at Beck. He was sound asleep. It was the most peaceful Falcon had seen him since the surgery. Falcon breathed a sigh of relief. With Beck on the mend, Falcon wouldn't feel as guilty about leaving them alone.

"Is this a video of supposedly straight Falcon Valspiro with a mystery *man*? Some fans seem to think so, as the video has gone viral, amassing more than..."

Falcon's heart stopped before racing into his throat. He spun and stared at the TV in shocked horror. Dillion had the remote pointed at the TV but seemed to be equally as frozen as an image of Falcon straddling Mason's lap at the gym filled the screen. The video played, damning him. Images of Falcon coaxing Mason to kiss him between sit-ups filled the entire gigantic screen that took up the wall inside Dillion's living room. Since he wore a ball cap, some might not recognize him. His face was partially hidden, but Dillion would know.

"Baby?"

Falcon glanced Beck's way at the quietly spoken word. Beck was awake, and it was obvious he recognized the oncoming storm.

Dillion turned. His gaze landed on Falcon. The betrayal in Dillion's eyes said it all. Without a word, he walked away. Falcon followed, but Dillion slipped inside the bedroom and closed the door before Falcon could explain. Not that he knew what to say.

Falcon pressed his forehead to the closed bedroom door. "Angel, please. Open the door." Silence met his plea. As much as Falcon wanted to beg for Dillion to hear him out, Falcon had no words. He didn't know how to explain something even he didn't understand. "It's fine. I'll go." Falcon headed for his room. Beck was home. Dillion didn't need him anymore. His phone vibrated in his back pocket. Text after text rolled in. Falcon watched them appear, feeling nothing.

Mom: *So you're gay now? I knew I shouldn't have let you hang out with that Dillion boy.*

Mason: *I didn't know anyone was watching. I thought we were alone.*

Mason: *Call me.*

Dad: *Marry Dillion right now and lock down that money. Don't squander this opportunity if you're switching teams.*

Mason: *I'm so, SO fucking sorry. Please, call me.*

Mason: *Jesus Christ. My phone is blowing up with texts from everyone but you.*

Brett: *Man, we got sponsors calling, wanting to know what's up. What do you want me to do?*

Falcon turned his phone off before he saw anything else. He grabbed his bags and started shoving things inside. There was a hum in his brain warning he would self-destruct soon. Falcon was always his own worst enemy when things started falling apart around him. He needed to disappear. Figure out his next move. He took a breath. Hyperventilating felt right around the corner. His head spun, but Falcon didn't stop moving. He was probably forgetting more than half his stuff. Fuck it. He would buy new stuff. Falcon headed down the hall.

"Falcon."

Falcon froze. Beck sounded like shit. He couldn't run out without making sure he was okay. He poked his head inside the living room. "Do you need anything before I go?"

Beck stared at him in silence, as if assessing the situation before shaking his head. "Tell Dillion I need him. He'll come out for that and then you can talk to him."

Unexpectedly, Falcon's throat swelled. He had done a terrible thing to his best friend, Beck was Dillion's fiancé, and yet Beck still tried to help.

Falcon understood why Dillion loved him. Falcon tried clearing his throat. It didn't work. His voice still cracked when he spoke. "I've told enough lies already, but thanks. Text him when I'm gone so he knows it's safe to come out and you're not stuck with no one to care for you, okay?"

"You don't have to leave."

"Yes I do," Falcon said before Beck could argue further. "But thanks. Get better, okay? Dillion needs you."

"He needs you too." Beck's claim came as Falcon walked away. Falcon didn't stop. Dillion didn't need him. Not anymore. It was best for Falcon to disappear now. There was nothing left here for him to break.

EIGHT

MASON STARED AT HIS PHONE, willing it to ring. He couldn't think straight anymore. That fucking video. They had been so much in their own bubble that they had honestly believed they were alone in that gym. He had clung to hope that Dillion hadn't seen. After all, Dillion never watched gossip television or bothered with social media. He hated all that bullshit, calling it a cesspool for bullies and liars. After calling and texting Falcon repeatedly with no response, Mason had finally accepted the truth—Dillion knew. Falcon would never forgive him.

The problem was, Mason was still sitting in Falcon's house, waiting for him to come home. Tuesday had come and gone. Wednesday had been hell. Now Thursday was upon him and Mason no longer knew what to do. What if Falcon was missing, hurt, or a million other things? What if he had gone to some secret location for a match and gotten hurt? He could be in an empty field right now and no one would know, because Mason was a fucking secret and trapped.

There was one option left to him. Mason stared at Dillion's number. All he had to do was press the little green phone symbol and he would know. Mason tapped the symbol. His eyes fell closed as he brought the phone to his ear. He listened to the ringing while his hands shook. Honest to God, he never meant for any of this to happen.

"Hello?"

"Don't hang up," Mason said much louder than he intended. He was too scared to temper his voice. "I need help."

He heard Dillion take a breath. "All right."

"Falcon is missing. At least, I think he is. Fuck," Mason breathed, hating everything about this. He cleared his throat. "I hoped, since that video went viral, you wouldn't be completely floored when I called, but I don't know who else to contact. But, I mean, you know Falcon. He could have—last minute—scheduled a fight and wound up hurt. I couldn't be the only person who knows and not say anything."

"Stop beating around the bush, Mason."

All right. His time was short, apparently. "I'm staying at his place in Vegas," Mason said the words fast, hoping to cause as little damage as possible. "and Falcon said he would be back from Aspen on Tuesday. It's Thursday, obviously, and he didn't come back. I've tried texting him, but he hasn't responded. When I call his cellphone, it goes straight to voicemail. Honestly, I don't know what to do. Since that video went viral, I don't know if he's avoiding me and I should just leave, or if he's hurt somewhere. God, I feel like a complete ass calling you, but I'm at a loss. Do I call the police or go home?"

A moment passed. In reality, it was probably only seconds, but it felt like forever before Dillion responded. "Just sit tight, okay? Let me check a few places and I'll call you back. Give me two hours before you call the police. Fair enough?"

Mason nodded, as if Dillion could see. "Yeah. That's fair. Thank you, Dillion. I know you're probably mad as hell and don't have to help me, but I appreciate it."

Dillion cleared his throat. "I'll do what I can. Two hours, okay?"

"Okay. Talk to you then." Mason disconnected the call and went back to staring at the wall. It was odd. He hadn't talked to Dillion in a long time. There had been a small part of him that worried how he would react when he did. He felt... sick over Falcon being missing, honestly. There was nothing in his heart for Dillion beyond being grateful he was willing to help despite the situation. Mason would give Dillion two hours and then... he didn't know. There was a voice in the back of his head, whispering Mason knew the truth. Falcon was somewhere, waiting for Mason to go home. That video was a nail in the coffin. They were over. Just as Falcon promised they would be if Dillion ever found out. His eyes fell closed. He would go home. It was time. Two hours from now, nothing would change. Falcon was done with him. It hurt every bit as much as he had expected. Too bad he was the only who cared.

THE FIRE CRACKLED AND POPPED. ITS ORANGE glow didn't bring Falcon peace. This cabin in the middle of nowhere used to be his sanctuary. Now, nothing felt right, especially his own skin. He hadn't turned his cellphone on since leaving Dillion's. Falcon wondered how many times Mason had called. Maybe Falcon was a bastard, but Mason had known that from day one. When the door flew open, Falcon sighed. He should have seen this coming.

"I love the way you knock." He knew it was Dillion without having to look. Not only did no one else know about this place, Falcon could pick out Dillion's footsteps in the dark and blindfolded. That was how well he knew his best friend.

"Please. Spare me. We haven't knocked at each other's homes since I was twelve. I don't intend to start now. Maybe you've decided it's cool to completely shit on our friendship, but I haven't."

Falcon rolled his eyes at Dillion's dramatics as Dillion peeled off his coat and sank down onto the opposite end of the couch. He glanced over. Dillion looked every bit as lovely as always. If he lost any sleep over Falcon, Dillion would never let it show. He was too good of an actor and too amazing at doing his makeup. "What brings you to Chateau Falcon?"

"Why are you hiding from Mason?"

Oh, that. He should have known Dillion wouldn't come to save them. "I'm not."

Dillion refused to look his way. Falcon couldn't

look anywhere else. He had always loved Dillion's eyes. "Well, what the hell are you doing, then? I know you're not hiding from me. That's impossible."

"I'm ruminating." Fuck if Falcon knew what he was doing. He had lost his mind a long time ago.

Dillion pulled a face that screamed Falcon was full of shit. He unwound his scarf and settled in. "I guess I'm ruminating with you then, until you stop being dumb."

"Prepared to die here, are you?"

An adorable-sounding growl fell from Dillion's lips. "Why do you get to sit in a cabin and pout? I'm the wronged party here."

"I don't know what you want to hear me say." Falcon didn't know anything anymore. He felt... bad. Like he was a bad person and he couldn't shake it.

"I want you to tell me why you're hiding from Mason. It's a little late to pull back now, don't you think? The deed is done. Don't try to tell me that you're hoping he'll take a hint and get out of your life. I saw that video. Several times, actually. I couldn't make myself stop watching it."

That confession had Falcon looking back Dillion's way. "Why?"

Dillion was the one who looked away this time. "Why are you always better than me?"

The question caught Falcon off guard. "What? What's that supposed to mean?"

Dillion growled again. He wrapped the scarf around his arm and stared at the fire. "Have you watched that video?"

"Why would I? I was there when it was made."

Dillion met his gaze. There was real hurt in his eyes and pain slammed into Falcon's chest. "He loves you. It was written all over his face in that video. I tried for what felt like forever to make Mason love me. Everyone always loves you. You're better than me in every way. There are seven billion people in this world, and you had to make that one love you better than he ever loved me, and I don't know how to handle it. You're straight, for fuck's sake, and you still loved him better than I could. I don't understand."

There was genuine pain in Dillion's voice and Falcon felt like the lowest piece of shit. Dillion wasn't wrong. Friends didn't do this to their friends. It was like—when it came to Dillion— Falcon was broken. The only way he could give Dillion peace was for Dillion to be done with him. "Do you remember the first time I brought you here?"

For a moment, Dillion stared at him in open

frustration before giving in. "Of course, I do. How could I forget?"

"It was your sixteenth birthday," Falcon said, as if Dillion hadn't just said he remembered.

Dillion nodded. "You bought me my first dress. I wore it for you. It was the first time anyone had ever made me feel normal. It was the best birthday I ever had."

Falcon hated he was about to ruin that memory. "It wasn't you I tried to make normal. I thought, as long as you wore that dress, I could still claim I was straight when I kissed you. If you were a girl on the inside, then I wasn't gay when I tugged down your panties and fucked your crack. As long as you wore that dress when you got on your knees, I was good. I got to tell myself for the past few years that I hadn't met a girl who could win me, because I'm in love with you, which doesn't make me gay, because it's you." Dillion didn't look like he could blink. His wide-eyed stare kept Falcon confessing his every sin. "Even when Mason crawled into my bed at Summer's wedding, thinking I was you, and I fucked him in a drug-induced haze, I got to tell myself I was out of my head. It wasn't on me. I had never touched another man before him. You don't count. I don't really remember that night and so I'm good. Every time after that, I told myself it was because he loves you. Like, I somehow had a piece of you through him. Baby, I'm not better than you at anything. I'm just really good at lying to myself."

Dillion looked away and stared at the fire. He wrapped his arms around his middle, as if barely holding himself together. A tear slid down his cheek. Falcon had never felt like a bigger piece of shit than he did in that moment. Only a bastard would make Dillion cry. Without a word, Dillion stood, gathered his things, and headed for the door.

"Call Mason," he said in a pained voice as he left Falcon alone with his guilty conscience.

With a deep breath for strength, Falcon dug out his phone. When he powered it up, he wondered if it would ever stop buzzing with incoming messages. Once it stopped, he didn't bother checking them. He called Mason. It rang four times before he answered, making Falcon wonder if Mason considered not answering.

"I see you're not dead."

Despite everything, Falcon settled deeper into the couch and smiled. The tightness in his chest eased at only the sound of Mason's voice. "What are you doing right now?"

"Sitting in the airport, waiting on a flight."

Falcon's eyes fell closed. "So you decided not to wait."

Even though it hadn't been a question, Mason answered. "Yeah. It seemed kind of pointless to stick around when you're obviously not coming home."

Falcon ran a hand through his hair. "Look, things went sideways here."

"Please don't." The softly spoken plea took Falcon's breath. He nodded. The move was for himself. He would stop.

"Yeah. Okay. I just wanted to let you know I'm not dead."

"Cool." Mason hung up.

Falcon dropped the phone and stared at the ceiling. This felt about right. Falcon was good at driving people away. So what if he thought he couldn't push Dillion away. Bad on him for thinking Mason would put up with anything. He had finally succeeded in his lifelong campaign to be completely alone in the world. It didn't feel like a win.

DILLION DROVE HOME, GETTING THERE BY muscle memory alone because his brain had no part in the trip. His chest hurt. All he wanted was to set eyes on Beck. Beck was his safe place. The steady center of his universe when everything else felt wrong. His rock. Dillion didn't breathe another full breath until his gaze landed on the love of his life.

Beck eyed him as he cleared the living room doorway. "You're home so much earlier than I expected."

Dillion flashed Beck a small smile. "It didn't take as long as I thought."

"I'm glad. Not only did I miss you, but I have to pee," Beck admitted with a laugh.

"Oh no. I'm so sorry, baby. I just rushed out to find Falcon without thinking. Let me help you." Dillion dropped everything to help Beck from the couch.

"It's no problem. After all, Falcon dropped everything to rush to your side while I was in the hospital."

Dillion didn't want to talk about Falcon. Beck had tried several times in the past few days to get Dillion to open up, but he just didn't have it in his spirit. First, Beck had almost died, and then everything had fallen apart in an instant with Falcon. Dillion was just spent. He helped Beck to the bathroom and paced outside the door until he was done. After he helped Beck back to the couch,

Dillion climbed in next to him. "Don't worry. I'll be careful. But I need to hold you."

Beck opened his arms to him. "I'm not worried about you hurting me. Your cuddles are worth it. Plus, I've missed holding my angel. It was horrible being stuck in the hospital. Now I'm stuck on the couch. I'm used to holding you while I sleep. This sucks."

Dillion snuggled as close as he could while avoiding Beck's wound. He buried his face in the crook of Beck's neck and inhaled. "Have I told you lately that you're my whole world?"

"Probably." There was a hint of laughter in Beck's voice. It warmed Dillion's heart, because he knew it was happiness that made Beck sound that way. He wanted his man to be even happier. More than that, he never wanted to lose Beck. Beck was the only person on the planet whose love didn't hurt.

"I want to get married."

Beck leaned away so he could see Dillion's face. He looked thoughtful. "Do you *want* to get married or are you upset about Falcon?"

"Can't both be happening at the same time?"

Beck didn't miss a beat. "Yes."

"Then I'm both," Dillion admitted. "But I had already decided I didn't want to wait anymore to get married before things fell apart with Falcon. I almost lost you. That can't happen. I want to be tied to you in every way. This is forever. Can we?"

"Of course. I've just been waiting on you to be ready."

Dillion didn't hesitate. "I'm ready." There wasn't an ounce of doubt in his heart. All Dillion had was Beck. He wanted to carry the man's last name and disappear with his husband for a while.

Beck pressed his lips to Dillion's temple and inhaled. For a long moment, they stayed like that. "Not everyone is as brave as you are," Beck said, proving he was always the smartest and most observant man in every room.

Dillion's eyes filled with tears. "I know, but it's because I have you."

"Who does Falcon have?"

Dillion wanted to say Falcon had him, but he didn't. Instead, he snuggled closer to Beck. The thing was, Falcon really didn't have him. Not anymore. There had been a time when Dillion dropped everything whenever Falcon called. Then, Dillion had found Beck. Falcon stopped calling. He should have known something was wrong, but Dillion wasn't sure he knew Falcon at all anymore. A growl escaped him before he could stop it from happening.

Beck kissed his temple again. "Do you mind grabbing me some water and a blanket before you go? That trip to the bathroom wore me out."

Damn. He loved Beck. There was no one else like him. He knew Dillion better than anyone else alive. Dillion wasn't the kind of person who stayed angry with anyone. Dillion was more likely to let people run all over him. If Falcon found happiness with Mason, then that was what had happened. Maybe Mason living here in Aspen would make Falcon finally move here. He loved Falcon. Dillion wanted him to be happy. Things went deeper than his best friend sleeping with his ex. What Falcon had said about Dillion's sixteenth birthday was all true. Back then, Dillion had been extremely confused by the combination of his sexuality and his desire to dress as a woman. There was a ton of pressure for him to fit in a certain box. No one had told him it was okay to be a feminine gay who was still a boy. Falcon's open willingness to let Dillion explore every side of himself had been freeing. But now, Falcon's confessions tainted that memory. Falcon had said those things to purposely hurt Dillion. To push him away. He had chosen Mason, whether he admitted it or not. It hurt. Not because Dillion's best friend loved his ex, but because Dillion had thought they were unbreakable.

Dillion scooted higher and kissed Beck, pouring all his love into the act. Beck's love was beautiful and unselfish. Dillion couldn't hold everyone to the standard Beck set. If everything that happened inside that cabin on Dillion's birthday helped Falcon come closer to accepting himself, then Dillion wasn't angry. It was a long time ago. Falcon was his friend. Sexuality was complicated sometimes. Everyone expected things to be cut and dry. They weren't. Sometimes, the heart wanted something completely unexpected. No amount of learning scientific scales could prepare a person for that.

"I love you," Dillion whispered between kisses. "Thank you for loving me exactly as I am, even on the days I don't know who that is."

"You make it easy." Beck sounded tired as hell. Dillion knew he needed to let Beck rest. He also needed to deal with Falcon. He kissed Beck one more time before rolling to his feet. Dillion made Beck a glass of water, grabbed him a blanket, and found his pain meds. He ensured Beck was fast asleep before heading out again. When he reached the car, Dillon remembered he hadn't called Mason.

He sent him a text instead since he was too upset to talk to Mason right then.

Dillion: *I found him. He's still here at a cabin in the middle of nowhere. My guess is he doesn't have cell service that deep in the mountains.*

That last part was a lie, but it wasn't Dillion's responsibility to dump Mason. If Falcon didn't want to be with Mason any longer, he could tell him his damn self.

Mason: *Thanks. He called. I'm already boarding my flight to go home, but I appreciate you letting me know.*

Dillion tilted his chin up and prayed for strength. As soon as Beck was well enough to travel, they were disappearing. He had been worn out from Mason's drama a long time ago. Dillion never dreamed he would be dealing with him again. He put the car in reverse. This time, he paid attention to the drive. Dillion let his anger grow with every passing mile, wrapping it around him like a shield. He didn't know if he could reach Falcon or if their friendship was over, but he would try to salvage what he could. By the time he reached the tiny secluded cabin again, Dillion was in battle mode.

Dillion stormed the door, holding his anger and love to his chest. He damn near kicked it open.

Falcon was sitting exactly where Dillion left him. Once again, Falcon didn't even look over his shoulder as Dillion used his fury to eat up the space between them. With the couch in the center of the living room, facing the fireplace, Dillion was free to attack Falcon from behind. He snagged the man around the neck and held on.

"Don't you ever fucking lie to me again to try drive me away and make it my fault for giving up. I'm so goddamn mad at you, but I know you better than anyone. You don't get to destroy our friendship to soothe your guilty conscience. I know you love me. I've always known you love me, but I also know damn well it's never been a romantic love." Falcon's chin dropped to Dillion's forearm. He held on and Dillion refused to stop. "I'm not your parents or some one-night stand you met at a club. This isn't some fair-weather friendship you get to walk away from. You've helped me through the worst times of my life and the first time you brought me here was no different." He tightened his hold on Falcon, letting him know he wasn't playing around. If Falcon wanted to be rid of him, he would have to physically throw him away. He pressed his lips to Falcon's temple. "If you love him, say it. I know you wouldn't have touched him if I had ever really loved him. I didn't. So, tell me the truth."

Falcon leaned into Dillion's touch. He pressed his lips to Dillion's arm. Silence dragged on between them. Dillion waited him out. He wasn't leaving until Falcon was honest. When Falcon finally spoke, his voice sounded horrible—like he had been chewing on glass. "I'm so sorry, baby. I don't know why I do the things I do."

Dillion fought the tears stinging his eyes. "Do you love him?"

Falcon nodded. His shoulders sagged. Dillion felt the life bleed from him. "Yes." It was the barest of whispers, but it sounded like gunfire to Dillion's ears.

Dillion's throat swelled. He never thought he would see the day that Falcon would love anyone in a romantic sense. Falcon didn't believe in love. It seemed love believed in him, though. Fuck. He hoped Mason didn't destroy Falcon the way he had Dillion. Dillion wished it had been anyone, anyone at all besides Mason, but his wants didn't matter. "Get your shoes and coat and let's go."

"Where?"

Dillion straightened his spine. "To get your man

before you fuck up everything beyond redemption. He's on his way home. You can wait for him there."

Falcon turned and met Dillion's stare. He looked every bit as wrecked as Dillion felt. "No. I won't choose him over us."

The burning in Dillion's throat increased. "I would never expect you to choose. Love doesn't work like that. I want you to be happy. That's it." Like it or not, Falcon loved Mason. Dillion would find a way to live with that, because Falcon meant more than the ache in Dillion's chest. Dillion saw that pain for what it was—fear of Falcon ending up hurt. Otherwise, he felt nothing about Falcon being with Mason. It didn't matter. Beck was his life now. Everything else in his life was just window dressing.

FALCON HELD HIS SILENCE ALL THE WAY TO Mason's house. It wasn't until they sat parked in Mason's driveway that Falcon lost the battle against himself.

"You're my friend, and he hurt you. How can you—"

"Hush," Dillion said, cutting him off. "You're my friend. That's loyalty talking. The truth isn't that simple." Dillion looked over and held his stare. "You love me, so I know you don't want to see me as I really am, but when I was with Mason, I was fucked up." Falcon couldn't ignore the power in Dillion's words. He hung on every syllable. "Growing up without parents who loved me fucked me up," Dillion said, emphasizing each word, and leaving Falcon speechless. "When I met Mason, I just wanted someone to love me. I didn't care who. I didn't care that he didn't want a child. Every time he told me we shouldn't be together until after I turned eighteen, I ignored his feelings. I thought, I was an emancipated adult, so his thoughts didn't matter. You know me, I'm spoiled. I wanted what I wanted and fuck everything else. I was desperate to have someone, anyone love me. No matter what. Meeting Beck saved me. People can say love doesn't save anyone. Real people need counseling. Well, fuck all that noise. *He saved me.* Beck set me free. He loves me just as I am and taught me to love myself." Dillion smiled. There wasn't an ounce of happiness in the gesture. "Mason did a lot of horrible shit to me, but I wasn't innocent. Everyone is the villain in someone's story. I know that you think Mason is mine, but I think—maybe—I'm also his. I kept him trapped." Dillion took a breath. It sounded ragged as hell. "The same way I've kept you a prisoner in my life." A tear rolled down Dillion's cheek. He wiped it away. "So I'm setting you both free."

Pain slammed into Falcon's chest, stealing his breath. "I don't want to be set free. You're my best friend. I need you."

More tears came, streaming without an end in sight. This time, Dillion didn't bother wiping them away. "You didn't do anything wrong. I did. You need time away from me, so—maybe—Mason can save you." Dillion took another breath. It was stuttered and the sound nearly wrecked Falcon. "You can't lose me." Dillion's chin shook as he made the claim. "But you need for me to let you go."

Falcon covered his mouth. He hadn't cried in years, but he was on the edge. His eyes burned. He couldn't breathe. Falcon sucked air. He tried to be strong. "I will always be only a phone call away. Nothing can change that."

"Same. Always. I promise you that you cannot lose me. Please, go get your happiness before it gets away."

Falcon lost the battle. Tears rolled down his cheeks. He swiped at them. He didn't want to be weak. Falcon had never felt less strong in his life. "I love you."

Dillion flashed him a watery smile. "I love you too." He shrugged. "Who knows? Maybe this will lead to me getting to see you more often. Now hug me, and then go fight for your man."

Falcon leaned across the car and towed Dillion into his arms. He felt it then. He couldn't lose Dillion. Their bond was too strong, even when Falcon didn't feel like he could carry everything. Now all he had to do was convince Mason that he wasn't a complete piece of shit. Unfortunately, even Falcon wasn't sure that was true. Maybe Mason would keep him anyway.

NINE

MASON DRAGGED his suitcase down the hall. He would unpack later. Right now, he was exhausted from the heartache and worry. He hadn't slept in days from wondering where Falcon had gone. Now he knew. They were over and that hurt, but at least he could sleep now, knowing Falcon was safe. He would go to bed and figure out his life later. In truth, nothing had changed. He still possessed the same amount he had before leaving for Vegas—nothing. Except now, he couldn't pretend otherwise. That was all Falcon had been anyhow—a fantasy. Mason should be used to that by now. Guys loved to slum it by fucking him, but they never had any interest in a real life together. Mason should have done the same thing with Falcon as he had done with Dillion—

protected his heart every step of the way. Instead, he had been stupid. It wouldn't happen again. Mason needed to focus on his life and nothing else now. That was how he would get through.

"For fuck's sake, did you book a flight home with six layovers? I didn't think you'd ever get here."

Mason's head shot up. He didn't realize he had been staring at his feet until Falcon spoke. Falcon sat in the center of Mason's bed, looking like the sexy wicked god he always did. Mason's chest hurt. "Getting a flight on short notice wasn't easy. I had to take what I could get." What he could afford, he silently added.

"I guess your vacation wasn't much of a vacation."

Mason shrugged while moving his suitcase out of the way. "It doesn't matter. I have all the time off I could possibly want now. My boss called and told me not to bother coming back. It seems having a video of me making out with a client at work go viral didn't go over well." He should be upset. Mason couldn't feel anything. He was numb. Logically, he realized the shock of losing too many things at once was getting to him. Mostly, he was just grateful for the reprieve to not feel.

"I'm sorry."

Mason peeled off his shirt. He didn't bother looking Falcon's way. "Don't bother. I'm not without options. Trace said he would always have a place for me at Incubus." He undid the button on his jeans. "Did I want to go back to working every weekend until four in the morning? No, but whatever. I'm pretty used to not having a life." Mason dug through the dresser, looking for clean clothes. He needed a shower. Mason felt like he was swimming in other people's germs after two airports and planes.

"Obviously, I feel bad about getting you fired, but that's not what I meant specifically. I'm sorry about everything."

No matter how much he tried, Mason still couldn't look Falcon's way. He kept his head down. "Fantastic." Even Mason heard the exhaustion in his voice. "Everyone looks forward to the day they're regretted. Look, I need a shower, and I'm tired as hell from staying awake worrying unnecessarily about you for the past few days. Everything is cool. From day one, I knew you would choose Dillion. I wouldn't want you to choose me over someone who's been your friend since you were little. If anyone knows I'm not worth keeping around, it's me. So, if you don't mind, I've been kicked enough for one lifetime. Now I just really want to get some sleep."

"Dillion dropped me off here, so you're kind of stuck with me."

Mason's gaze finally lifted at that one. "I'm... confused."

Falcon's shoulder lifted in a half shrug. "You should go take your shower. I'm not going anywhere."

With his bottom lip between his teeth, Mason shuffled from one foot to the other. He didn't want to hope. Hope always took his knees out with a sledgehammer.

"Go," Falcon said, motioning for him to scoot.

"I'm afraid to take my eyes off you before I get an explanation." The admission came from Mason's soul. He didn't want to lose this chance.

Falcon's heart was in his eyes. "I swear I won't move from this spot."

With a nod, Mason headed for the bathroom. He tried to hurry, but he kept catching himself staring into space lost in thought. Falcon was so beautiful. He looked like an angel while sitting on Mason's bed. Mason just wanted to be with him. In his company. That was all. He was tired of being alone. Falcon made him feel alive. Now Mason felt empty and spent. He had to know why Falcon was here. The sooner he knew, the better for his sanity.

His skin was still damp, and water dripped from his hair to his shoulders as he pulled on a pair of pajama pants. The sun had barely set, but Mason couldn't focus on anything but his bed and the man in it. By the time he made it back out to the bedroom, Falcon was curled onto his side, facing the wall. Incapable of stopping himself, Mason crawled onto the bed and scooted as close as he could get to Falcon's back, until he could drape his arm over Falcon's body.

Falcon snuggled closer. "Mason." Falcon sounded half asleep.

Mason didn't want to wake him. He wanted to hold him one more time. "Hmm?"

"You don't have to worry about getting fired. I love you. I won't let anything bad happen to you."

Mason tried to breathe around Falcon's confession. "Losing my job was nothing. It's losing you that's killing me. I didn't mean to fall in love with you. I know you didn't want that."

Falcon rolled in his arms and pressed his cheek to Mason's chest. "You haven't lost me. Unless you've decided you don't want me any longer. As for your love, I absolutely want that. That's mine."

Mason wanted to be happy, but he had gotten so used to being scared, he didn't know how to trust this. He held Falcon to his chest. His fingers trailed up and down Falcon's spine. Neither of them rushed to do anything more. It was a quiet acceptance that grew in power by the moment. Mason had so many questions, he didn't know where to start. Except one question kept rising to the top.

"Why do all these gossip sites keep calling you supposedly straight?"

Falcon chuckled against his skin. The sensation made Mason's eyes sting. He hadn't thought he would ever hold Falcon again. Mason had never been so scared. He loved Falcon. For real. What he felt for Falcon put everything he had ever experienced to shame.

"Um," Falcon hummed against his chest. "Well, since we're baring our souls, you're the only guy I've ever dated."

Mason tried wrapping his mind around that one. He cleared his throat. To some degree, that explained a few things. "Am I the only guy you've dated publicly, or am I the only guy you've been with period?"

Falcon shifted. He clung a little tighter to Mason. "Do you really want to know this?"

Did he? "Yes."

"The only other guy I've ever touched in any

way that could be loosely deemed as sexual is Dillion."

"Why me?"

"Because you looked like you felt every bit as lonely as me at Summer's wedding." Falcon's words came out sounding half asleep.

"Wait... what?"

Falcon's entire body jerked like Mason woke him the exact moment he drifted to sleep. "What? What's wrong, baby?"

Mason lightly pushed Falcon away so he could see the man's face. He looked like hell. Mason heart squeezed in his chest. He wondered how long it had been since Falcon slept. Still, he had to know. "Did you end up in my room on purpose at Summer's wedding?"

Falcon blinked. His beauty always tried stealing Mason's resolve. "Yes."

Mason was speechless.

Luckily, Falcon didn't leave things there. "In my defense, I didn't intend to pass out and not remember anything. That part was an accident. Honestly, I don't know what I wanted that night. Not to be alone anymore, I guess. You were staring at Dillion. I was watching you. It just hit me in the chest, I suppose."

Wow. Mason tried wrapping his mind around that. He wasn't angry or upset. Just blown away really. There was no end to the surprises with Falcon. He kissed Falcon's forehead. "Go to sleep, sexy." He tugged the blankets up and snuggled close. "Everything will still be waiting for us in the morning."

Falcon nodded against his chest. He clung to Mason like a lifeline. "I love you."

Mason's body immediately relaxed. His breathing deepened. It was amazing how a single claim from Falcon put him at ease. They would be okay. This was meant to be. In the morning, they would figure out their next move. Whatever it was, it would be together. Mason felt that in his soul.

Falcon's entire body jerked again—like he had startled awake again. "Mason." There was a hint of panic in Falcon's voice. In an instant, Falcon's entire body began to shake. Mason flew into nurture mode. He patted Falcon down, looking for a problem. "What's wrong, baby?"

Falcon couldn't even talk from the chattering of his teeth. He locked his jaw and stared at Mason through wild eyes. Pure fear kicked Mason into action. He dove for the phone, calling the only person he could think to call for help.

Dillion answered on the second ring. "Hello?"

"Something's wrong with Falcon." Even Mason heard the hysteria in his voice.

"Tell me."

"He dozed off and kind of startled himself awake. Now his jaw is locked, and he's shaking all over."

"Oh, dear. I should've seen this coming. It's okay. He has a panic disorder. When he's under extreme stress, he has bad panic attacks. He can't control it. Um. You'll have to get in his face and force him to hold your stare. Breathe with him, taking deep, steady breaths. Just try to keep him calm. If he stays tensed up for too long, he might end up with a migraine afterward. If that happens, text me and I'll bring over his meds."

"Thank you. I'll try that."

"It's no problem. Keep me posted."

After promising to call later, Mason tossed his phone aside and did as Dillion said. He crawled into bed next to Falcon and held Falcon's face between his hands, forcing Falcon to hold his stare. "It's okay, baby. I'm right here. Breathe with me." He took a deep breath in through his nose, trying to coax Falcon to do the same. Falcon's entire body heaved as if it took every ounce of his effort to suck in a breath.

It looked painful, but Mason still praised him. "That's it, gorgeous. Keep breathing. I love you. You're so strong."

"Love you." Falcon still shook from head to toe, but the wave of relief was epic at the sound of Falcon's voice.

Mason rubbed Falcon's arm and held Falcon's stare. Goddamn. He really loved this man. He wasn't sure there was any revelation Falcon could drop on him that would drive him away, and damn, he had been hit with a few of those today. "Why didn't you warn me about the panic attacks?"

A muscle jumped in Falcon's cheek as he struggled against the shaking. "Don't like being weak."

"Oh, baby. You're not weak." Mason stroked Falcon's jaw with the backs of his knuckles, trying his damnedest to help Falcon calm down. He swore he could see Falcon's heart racing. "You're the strongest man I've ever met. Seriously, you put everyone I know to shame. You take care of everyone and never complain. I don't know how you're not exhausted and fed up. You have a beautiful soul. I'm so proud to have your love."

Falcon's chest rose and fell, doing a much better job of breathing. "I'm so sorry for failing everyone."

A sad smile tugged at Mason's lips. "Stop trying to be perfect and everything to everyone and just be happy. That's all the people who love you expect. It's not your job to please everyone." The longer Mason spoke, the more Falcon relaxed. "Tell me how I can make you better."

Falcon surprised him by not hesitating. "Kiss me."

Mason moved slow and tried to be gentle. He could still feel a slight quiver running through Falcon as he brushed his lips across Falcon's mouth. His hand automatically pushed Falcon's shirt up, going for bare skin. Mason couldn't help himself. It was like he was incapable of kissing Falcon without feeling the man's soft skin beneath his fingertips. Falcon stayed still, accepting every touch. His lips parted. Their tongues met. Everything else fell away. Mason found himself crawling closer until he straddled Falcon's body. He sat back on his heels and peeled away Falcon's shirt before going back for more kisses. His hands didn't rest. Mason tore open the front of Falcon's pants. Even though Mason's body was on fire. To his mind, this wasn't about sex. Mason needed the connection of their nude bodies— to be as close as possible to the heartbeat he had almost lost.

Until they were both completely unclothed, and Mason covered Falcon's body, Mason didn't draw another easy breath. Then, oxygen filled his lungs, making his head spin.

"I won't do anything. I just need to feel you."

Falcon's short fingernails dug into Mason's sides as he pulled him closer. "You'd better be willing to do something. I can't make the same promise."

A chuckle escaped Mason as their lips met. He knew Falcon had to still feel terrible, but Falcon wasn't letting that hold him back. Falcon felt like heaven beneath Mason. He was Mason's home. Mason didn't understand why they had gravitated toward one another. Maybe they were simply another example of the universe's twisted sense of humor. Mason didn't care if the joke was on him. He had Falcon. It felt a lot like winning.

"Tell me what you want so I can make it yours."

At Falcon's demand, Mason didn't hold back. "You. I just want to be with you."

"Done," Falcon said as he changed angles and deepened their kiss.

Mason didn't know what would happen tomorrow, but tonight, they were together. It was enough.

FALCON WANTED TO CRAWL BENEATH MASON'S skin so he could be an inch closer to his heart. His insides still shook, making him feel sick, but he had Mason. That was all that mattered. If all Mason wanted was him, Falcon would make sure it happened. Starting tomorrow, he planned to completely take over Mason's life. Right now, he needed to be as close as he could get. His heart required reassurance. Falcon wanted a million things all at once. His body craved release while his mind demanded they talk all night so his soul could rest easy. Then Mason's hips rolled and his erection ground against Falcon's. The air disappeared from Falcon's lungs. He turned his head away and sucked air, trying hard to breathe.

Mason's teeth scraped Falcon's throat. "I've never touched another soul in any way sexually without a condom. With you, it's like I can't stand the thought of anything at all between us."

Falcon got it. It was like they were one person, constantly searching for a way to merge and be whole. "Don't stop." There was no controlling the neediness. Almost losing Mason left Falcon feeling like nothing was right. More of Mason was the only cure.

Mason's teeth sank into Falcon's skin. A loud moan tore through the air. Falcon's body was on fire. He moved restlessly beneath Mason, searching for relief. "Tell me how to make you better."

"Don't stop touching me."

At his plea, Mason reached between them. He palmed their cocks, holding them in place as he thrust. A frisson of pleasure vibrated through Falcon. He bit Mason's shoulder and then sucked. The move was almost primal. He wanted to brand Mason's skin. Mark his territory. Falcon was almost desperate for the world to understand this one man was his.

Falcon's skin itched, feeling too tight. He focused on the sensations dancing on his dick. His hips lifted, searching for more. Falcon licked and sucked every place he could reach, savoring Mason's flavor. Images flashed through his mind. He was bent over the edge of Mason's bed while Mason took him—hard. It was crazy how much he wanted to try with Mason. Maybe he had been denying himself too much for too long. Or maybe love had changed him. Either way, he wanted to spend the rest of his life finding himself with Mason.

Pressure crawled up Falcon's shaft, stealing away

his thoughts. He gasped for air as he fought to reach a new height. Falcon thought he might scream in frustration. His body begged for more. The air lodged in Falcon's lungs as he strained to get where he wanted to go. An orgasm ripped through him. A cry burst from his lips. His heels dug into the mattress as he rode out the ecstasy.

"I love you. Oh, God. Don't stop."

Mason pumped and thrust. Sweat coated his skin. His mouth came down hard on Falcon's as more cum filled the space between them. Falcon could feel Mason's cock jumping and twitching against his. They were beautiful. This was the most important relationship in his life now. He understood Dillion's need to lock himself away with Beck better than ever before. Falcon craved this light filling him. He would go to any length or sink to any low to hang on to this. For the first time in Falcon's life, he couldn't wait to see what came next.

TEN

"ARE YOU READY TO DO THIS?"

Falcon nodded. He was ready. Today was the day. Mason rubbed Falcon's arms. Concern etched his features. Falcon's heart squeezed in his chest. "I love you."

The deep line between Mason's eyebrows disappeared, clearing away his frown. "I love you too. Let's go find Roman."

They linked fingers and headed for the kitchen hand in hand. Falcon hadn't done a single recording, live shoot, or anything publicly since that video had gone viral. That ended today. But first, they needed to iron out the final details. Falcon drew a steady breath, stealing comfort from the sensation of Mason's palm against his. He loved Mason too much to stay hidden.

His withdrawal into Mason's home and out of the public eye wasn't all about coming out. The biggest thing was solidifying their relationship, building something unbreakable. Falcon had other people counting on him as well. It was time to get moving.

They found Roman cooking, of course. Roman hadn't lied about nonstop eating. It was a bit ridiculous. Gluttony aside, Falcon had come to really like the guy. He hadn't once complained about Falcon holing up in his home for the past three months. Falcon couldn't let that pass without showing his gratitude.

Roman looked their way as they ventured into the kitchen. "Hey, guys. Did the smell of food coax you from your room?"

"Nah. We're about to head out," Mason answered for the both of them. "We wanted to talk to you first, though."

Roman's eyebrows rose. He reached over and turned the knob, killing the eye on the stove. "What's up? Are you finally ready to put me out?"

"No," Falcon said, rushing to stop any panic before it started. He had worried about this, since—technically—the house was in Mason's name. "It's the opposite, actually. I've had my manager, Brett, working on buying a place for us near Dillion. He's on his way to bring me the keys now, but I... we don't want you to worry, so I also paid off this house too, so you'll always have a place to stay."

Roman looked thunderstruck. Before he could respond, the back door opened, and Brett strolled in like he owned the place. That was Brett in a nutshell. He bowled people over without apology.

His gaze was locked on a stack of papers in his hand. He glanced up for half a second as he cleared the door. "Hey, guys. I hope you're ready for a full day." He finally scanned the room with his gaze, stopping briefly to eye Roman from head to toe. "Hello."

"Um. Hi," Roman said, visibly taken aback by Brett—the way everyone always was. He was tiny and beautiful. Brett was a stylish mess in full bright make-up. Today, he was like a small pride parade with rainbow eyeshadow. It was obvious he took his duty of introducing Mason to the world as a personal responsibility. Roman stared like every thought had been sucked from his head. Brett had that effect on men.

Roman dragged his gaze away from Falcon's pixie-sized manager to focus on Falcon once more.

"You didn't have to pay off the house. I could've found someplace else."

"No," Falcon argued. "I'm stealing your roommate. The least I can do is make sure you don't struggle because of it. Plus, you've been nothing but welcoming to me. So suck it up."

"I get the feeling this one always lands on his feet," Brett said under this breath, surprising Falcon. Falcon had never seen Brett hate anyone on sight, but he worried he was seeing it now with Roman. It was... odd.

Roman's gaze slid back Brett's way at the comment. "What's that supposed to mean?"

Brett didn't look the least bit chastised. "You look like a survivor. That isn't an insult," Brett added before Roman could get the wrong idea.

Falcon wasn't as sure, but he didn't have time to delve into an argument. He focused on Roman once more. "Anyhow, I know you're in the middle of something, but would you like to head over to the new place with us? I'm doing a live event while we're there. Dillion and Beck are meeting us too."

Roman looked between them. He swiped his palms on his jeans. "Um, yeah. I guess."

Mason slapped him across the back and used the momentum to steer Roman toward the door. "Don't worry. You'll get used to being swept away by the tide."

Falcon bit back a chuckle. Soon he would have all his friends in one place. He hoped he didn't puke. His nerves were already stretched beyond frayed. Then Mason's hand slid across the small of his back and everything was okay. He was grabbing the life he wanted with both hands. His gaze slid Mason's way. Everything would be okay.

MASON TOOK A BRACING BREATH AS BRETT silently counted down the seconds, taking Falcon live. Even though he was out of the line of the camera's view, he was nervous as hell on Falcon's behalf. Most people were never forced to this extreme of coming out. It was another reason to add to the list of reasons why he hoped—someday soon—people weren't forced to announce their sexuality at all. Falcon wouldn't get to move past this until he did. He lived too much under a microscope to stay silent and let rumors build. It was no wonder Falcon had been scared to deal with his sexuality. No one should have to endure this.

The countdown ended and Falcon smiled.

Mason was so goddamn grateful for the man standing at Falcon's side, holding Falcon's waist in front of the world. Dillion was a great human. Mason would never forget it.

"Hey, guys. I know it's been a few months since I've been around, but things have been insane on my end. Today, I've finally managed to wrangle everyone together in one place to address everything that's been going down." He motioned Dillion's way. "Dillion doesn't really need an introduction, but I'm giving him one anyway. You see, we grew up together. Most people didn't realize until a few years ago, when I started this channel, that we grew up side by side in front of the entire world. I was Dillion's stunt double in a series of nine blockbuster movies. We spent almost every day of our entire childhood together. He is more than my best friend. Dillion is and always will be the biggest part of me and the greatest love of my life." Dillion kept his gaze locked on Falcon, hanging on every word. His eyes filled with tears, but he blinked them away. Mason was just so damn grateful, he didn't know where to go with it. Things could have turned out so differently. Falcon kept pushing forward and Mason's nerves were ready to snap on his behalf. "Today, I get to introduce Dillion for the first time to the world by his new name. That's right. Apologies to all the broken-hearted, but Dillion is officially off the market. He is now Dillion Jackson, proud husband to Beckett Jackson." He motioned toward where Beck leaned against the wall in the background.

"There's Beck. He's a great guy. I won't force him to hang out in front of the camera. He hates that. Oh, the tall guy next to him with all the hair is Roman." Roman and Beck waved, looking oddly at ease. Falcon kept going as the camera came back to rest on him. "Roman is my other half's best friend, which brings me to my next point." His chest expanded on a deep breath. "I have lived my life so publicly the last few years that I didn't truly realize I kept part of my life hidden until a certain video went viral three months ago. Before then, I hadn't considered a lot of things. As much as I believe there are parts of my life I should be allowed to keep private, I don't want anyone to think I'm hiding anything. I'm not perfect. In fact, the people closest to me have deserved a lot better from me than they've gotten in—at least—the past year. That's why everyone I love the most is here today, even my manager, Brett. He's manning the camera."

Brett turned the camera his way and waved to

the world before turning the device back toward Falcon.

Falcon crossed the room, moving Mason's way. The camera followed him. Mason couldn't look away. "This is Mason," Falcon said, flashing Mason a smile before moving to stand at Mason's side. Their hands met. Mason couldn't look away from Falcon. He was so goddamn strong. "He's the other piece of me that I can't live without. While he's never complained about our relationship, he really has gotten screwed out of having a normal life with me. He hasn't been taken on dates or shown off to the world. If he resents it, he's never said a word. In fact, until that video went viral, I didn't think about how much he's missed because he fell in love with me."

He looked so sad. Mason wished he could fix it.

Falcon flashed him another smile, as if drawing strength from Mason's presence. "I didn't get to introduce Mason to the world before that video stole that from us. Funnily enough, though, after seeing that video a million times in the last three months, I'm not sure there is anything I could've done or said that would've done a better job of showing how much I love him." Falcon's chest expanded again. "But I'm about to try. This is our new home. We'll start moving in later today. From now on, the two of us will be sharing our lives, and everywhere I go, he'll be there. So get used to seeing his sexy face."

A startled chuckle escaped Mason before he could stop it. He loved this man so fucking much. It was hard to wrap his mind around it some days. Falcon had given him everything. Every time he thought there was nothing else Falcon could possibly do to blow him away, Falcon found something new.

As he watched Falcon drop to one knee, Mason realized today would be no different. He stared up at Mason with his heart in his eyes. Mason could barely breathe. "I haven't shown you off to the world like you deserved, but I brought the world and our closest friends to you so I could remedy that. Mason Jacobs, you've already agreed to share your life with me, but I still want more. I'd like to submit my application to be your husband."

A bark of laughter burst from Mason at Falcon's choice of words for proposing. Maybe this was as public as possible, but he had still found a way to make it completely personal with a reference only they would understand. "You're hired."

Their friends' laughter made a beautiful moment even better as Falcon came to his feet. Mason hauled Falcon into his arms and captured his mouth, uncaring of who witnessed their love. They had started as a secret, but they had always been perfect to Mason. He would accept Falcon in any capacity as long as they lived and as long as they were together. He was completely enamored by this slightly salty and extremely perfect man. Mason couldn't wait to start working on their forever life. He would never forget how much acceptance it had taken on everyone's part to get them here. Falcon was his happy ending.

Please consider leaving a review at the retailer where this book was purchased. Reviews really help with a book's visibility, which ensures I can continue writing. Thank you, Charity.

ABOUT THE AUTHOR

Charity Parkerson is an award winning and multi-published author with several companies. Born with no filter from her brain to her mouth, she decided to take this odd quirk and insert it in her characters.

*Eight-time Readers' Favorite Award Winner
   *2015 Passionate Plume Award Finalist
   *2013 Reviewers' Choice Award Winner
   *2012 ARRA Finalist for Favorite Paranormal Romance
   *Five-time winner of The Mistress of the Darkpath

Connect with her online:

--Join my street team: facebook.com/TeamCharityParkerson
   --Website: charityparkerson.com
   --Facebook: facebook.com/authorCharityParkerson

facebook.com/TheMenofSin

--Twitter: twitter.com/CharityParkerso